STILL THE BEST
WOMAN FOR THE JOB

SHARON C. COOPER

STILL THE BEST WOMAN FOR THE JOB

Copyright © 2013 Sharon C. Cooper

Book Cover: MTheresa Art Designs

Editor: Yolanda Barber, Write Time Write Place

Formatted by IRONHORSE Formatting

Published by: Amaris Publishing LLC in the United States

Please be advised that this story has adult and sensitive content not recommended for those under the age of 18.

ISBN: 0-9855254-9-5
ISBN-13: 978-0-9855254-9-1

DEDICATION

To the man I married, my best friend and the love of my life –
Al, thank you for your unconditional love and unwavering
support.
I love you more than I could ever express.

ACKNOWLEDGEMENTS

Special thanks to my amazing editor who helped this book see the light of day.

Dear Reader

I enjoy reading books that are a part of a series, and now I find that I enjoy writing them as well. Join me as I introduce you to a few members of the Jenkins family.

Steven Jenkins, the patriarch of the Jenkins family, and founder of Jenkins & Sons Construction wants what every entrepreneur head of the family wants - for his children to continue to run the family business long after he's dead and gone. None of his four sons and three daughters are interested in taking over the reins. It's not until his oldest granddaughter, Peyton Jenkins, shows an interest that his hope is renewed.

Now its 16 years later, he's happily retired, and business is better than ever - thanks to his five amazing granddaughters. Toni (TJ) Jenkins, a master plumber, is his favorite granddaughter - though he'll never admit it; Jada (JJ) Jenkins is the youngest and the most spirited of the bunch. Steven still hasn't been able to figure her out, but he has to admit, she's a darn good sheet metal worker. Then there's Christina (CJ) Jenkins, the shy one in the group and the most compassionate. She's a painter, but refers to herself as an artist. Martina (MJ) Jenkins, is a carpenter and Steven's most challenging grandchild who keeps everyone on their toes. Last, but not least, is sweet, levelheaded Peyton (PJ) Jenkins - an electrician and the senior construction manager for Jenkins & Sons Construction.

I hope you enjoy book 1 of the Jenkins Family Series – *Still the Best Woman for the Job*.

All the best to you,

Sharon C. Cooper

CHAPTER ONE

"Would you come on," Toni Jenkins gasped for air. "Put your back into it, Jada. How can you lug sheet metal around all day and can't help drag a sloppy drunk to the bathroom?"

Jada's chest heaved and her long, dark hair whipped across her face. She glared around Ronald's body at Toni. "Say one more thing and I will drop his heavy ass right here in the middle of the hallway. Then see how far you get in hiding him. Grampa's going to kill you when he finds out you're hanging out with drunks and that you brought one of them to his birthday party!"

Toni clamped her mouth shut and pulled the hem of her short dress down with one hand while she held onto her date, Ronald, with her other. She needed Jada's help. The last thing she wanted is for her grandmother to find out Ronald barfed on an eight-foot Golden Cane Palm Tree, one of her prize possessions. No, she couldn't handle a lecture tonight, but if her grandfather got wind of the night's events, that's exactly what she would get.

Character is built by the choices we make, her grandfather's familiar words taunted.

"Wha ... what are yo ... you doin' to me," Ronald slurred before his head dipped to the side and a low snore rumbled against Toni's ear.

"Oh, shut up," she mumbled under her breath.

What did her recent dating choices say about her character? Ronald might have been tall, good-looking and possessed a body women fantasized about, but he wasn't the brightest bulb on the Christmas tree. If she were honest with herself, she'd have to admit that she'd dated her share of losers since breaking up with Craig.

Argh! Why can't I stop thinking about him?

As soon as the question leaped into her mind, so did the answer. She was still in love with Craig Logan ... and she hated it. *Okay, stop thinking about him. Don't think about him, don't think about—* "Oh crap." Toni grabbed hold of the nearby wall when her foot slipped and she lost her grip on Ronald.

Her cousin glared at her. "If you don't..." she started but didn't finish when Toni regained her footing and grasped the back of Ronald's shirt, bringing him upright again. Thankfully, the bathroom was in sight and none of the party guest had found their way to the back of the house. The area was empty and quiet, perfect for hiding a body.

When they finally wrangled Ronald into the bathroom, both she and Jada collapsed against the cool, marbled tiled wall, Ronald's limp body propped up between them.

"Just think, only a Jenkins' girl could pull a two hundred pound man from a crowded ballroom and drag him through Gramma and Grampa's house wearing cocktail dresses and stilettos without anyone being the wiser," Jada wheezed.

"You're right." Toni closed her eyes, breathing heavily.

Thanks to their grandfather for encouraging her and her female cousins to pursue a career in the construction trades, Toni was now a master plumber. A career in plumbing seemed like the perfect solution after dropping out of college. Not only had she finished her apprenticeship five years ago, but she had also attended night school to complete her degree in mechanical engineering.

"I know this is a fine time to ask, but why did we bring him into the bathroom instead of dumping his butt in the backyard until he sobers up?"

Toni glanced at the bathroom door thinking she should probably close it, but was too tired to move. "We can't just chuck him outside and leave him. Hopefully he'll come to, but in the meantime, I need to clean him up so we can put him in the car and take him home."

"*We?*" Jada's voice raised an octave. She moved away from the wall but stopped when Ronald's body started sliding. "You are crazy in your head if you think I'm dragging him anywhere else! Look at me." With a flourish of her free hand, she brought attention to her short, Michael Kors dress. "Do you have any idea how much I paid for this outfit? I'm not about to let some boneheaded drunk throw up on me. I say we dump his butt on the floor and go get Johnny and the guys to throw him in the back of one of their trucks."

Toni liked the idea, but didn't know where her male cousins were hiding out. She hadn't seen them since they'd showed up at the party, late. It was safe to assume they were somewhere watching a basketball game since the NBA finals had just started.

"Okay, let's slowly slide his body down the wall and onto the floor." Toni bent her knees and they eased him along the tile, which wasn't easy to do in stilettos and a tight dress. "Almost there just ... oh no! Jada grab him!" Too late. Ronald's body jerked, Toni's arms flailed and the three of them crashed to the floor in a heap.

"Aaarrrgh!" Jada shrieked. Caramel toned arms and legs flapped around in distress under the weight of Ronald's body sprawled on top of Jada, his boozed breath in her face. "Oh my God! Oh my God! Get him off me! I think he just drooled on my dress," she screamed. "Toni, I'm going to kill you!"

***

Craig Logan pulled up to the Jenkins' family estate, a colossal brick home that expanded half the block located in the Village of Indian Hill, a suburb of Cincinnati. A mere representation of the Jenkins's wealth, the house stood out with every light shining through the cathedral style windows and illuminated the sky like fireworks on the fourth of July. Craig's fingers gripped the steering wheel tighter, and he willed the mounting anxiousness in his gut to loosen up. Knowing he'd see Toni soon brought mixed feelings. On one hand, he couldn't wait to see her, but on the other he wasn't sure he wanted to put himself through the torture of seeing her without being able to hold her in his arms.

He pulled onto the property. Luxury cars lined either side of the circular driveway that easily accommodated fifty cars. It wasn't until he noticed vehicles lining the paved driveway along the side of the house that he knew this was no small gathering, but what had he expected?

The Jenkins family, well known across the state of Ohio, had probably invited everybody who's anybody to the celebration.

He parked his car at the very end of the driveway, but didn't make a move to exit the vehicle still unsure of whether or not showing up was a good idea. When Toni's cousin, Peyton, insisted on him stopping by, saying how much the family had missed seeing him, he thought attending the party was a good idea. But now, he wasn't so sure.

His cell phone rang and he slowly dug the iPhone out of his pocket, debating on whether or not to answer. He was already late, and it wouldn't take much for him to change his mind about the party despite the fact that he'd driven forty-five minutes to get there.

He glanced at the cell phone screen and smiled. "Hello."

"What's up bro?"

"Hey man, what's going on?"

The sound of his brother's voice was a welcomed distraction. Two years older, Derek was more than his big brother he was also his best friend.

"Not too much, did I catch you at a bad time?" Derek asked.

"Actually I was just sitting here trying to force myself to go into Toni's grandfather's birthday celebration."

"Oh yeah, I forgot that was tonight. Why were you debating whether or not to go in? You already told Peyton you would be there and besides, I know you want to see Toni."

Craig traced the ridged lines on the steering wheel with his index finger, going in and out of the grooves thinking about the night he and Toni parted ways. *I can't handle dating a cop,* she had told him through her tears. *That could have been you.*

Craig and his partner of three years were both shot during a domestic violence call. He survived, but his partner hadn't. Craig would never forget that hot summer night, neighbors screaming and blood everywhere. It wasn't until he was lying in a hospital bed, with Toni by his side that his sergeant told him Julien hadn't survived. Craig remembered holding Toni in his arms providing as much comfort to her as he could offer, considering he had just lost one of his best friends.

"You're right," he finally said to his brother, "I do want to see her, but I don't know if I can handle being that close to her and then just walk away afterwards." He used his familiar I'm-in-control voice, but at this moment nothing was further from the truth.

"So you're still in love with her?" his brother asked.

"You know I am." Craig toyed with the car keys that dangled from the ignition. He thought dating other women would take his mind off Toni. If anything, dating others made him want her that much more.

"Well, I guess you know what you have to do." His brother's voice permeated his thoughts.

Craig kneaded the tight knot that formed between his eyes. "And what's that?"

"Give up the badge."

He dropped his hand and pounded the steering wheel. "Damn, Derek, you act as if sacrificing my career is easy." The knot in his stomach tightened. There wasn't much he wouldn't do for Toni, but what he did for a living meant so much more than just carrying a badge.

"Being willing to sacrifice your career is easy if Toni means as much to you as you say she does. Craig, it's not like you're hurting for money. When Uncle Sammy left you that house and enough money to do whatever the hell you wanted, I thought you would quit the force then."

Craig tensed in his seat. "Being a cop is not about the money and you know it! I shouldn't have to give up a job I love and one that I'm damn good at because Toni's afraid I might die in the line of duty."

Derek hesitated." Are you sure that's why you're still on the force? Or are you still fighting those demons? Trying to rid the streets of every single thug, whose goal in life is to attack and rape defenseless women."

Craig gripped his cell phone tighter and clenched his jaw as he willed himself not to react to his brother's words. Since the night he'd received the phone call that his fiancée had been raped and killed, he vowed to do everything in his power to make sure it didn't happen to any other woman. And then when he met Toni and found out she had gone through a similar experience in college, his being a cop took on a whole different meaning. He had to do whatever he could do to protect the female population from bastards who thought they had a right to abuse women.

"Listen, I'm not trying to piss you off, but I think it's time you realize that you are just one man. As sick as this reality may be, there will always be some butthole running the streets with evil intent. You can't stop or catch them all."

Craig rolled his shoulders and took a cleansing breath. He knew he couldn't stop them all, but he sure as hell could try.

"Hey, I didn't call to preach to you, but I did call to see if Jason and I could stay with you for a few days."

Craig's mood lightened at the mention of his three-year-old nephew, of whom his brother had sole custody. "You know you don't have to ask. You guys are always welcome."

"Good. We need a break from the renovations. The contractors have finished the upstairs bathroom, and now started on the kitchen. I can't take the chaos anymore."

Craig chuckled. "I warned you that remodeling was going to be a pain. I'm surprised you lasted this long. You and my nephew can stay as long as you need to."

Growing up in Columbus, Craig knew he didn't want to live there all his life, so when Derek relocated to Cincinnati, he did too. They now lived about twenty-five minutes from each other and hung out as often as possible.

"Great. I'm thinking we'll get there Wednesday and stay a few days or a week at the longest."

"Sounds good to me. Stay as long as you want."

"And Craig …"

"Yeah."

"Go to the party. Toni's missing you probably as much as you're missing her. Besides, if she's there, I'm sure she'll do something or has done something that will require you to bail her out of a situation." His brother laughed and then ended the call.

Craig grinned. Derek was right. Toni did have a way of getting herself into tight jams.

***

Toni chuckled as she tugged on one of Ronald's arms, at first unable to budge him off her cousin, but eventually rolling him away, just enough for Jada to scurry from under him. Toni crawled to the side and clamped her hand on the edge of the claw-foot tub for support as she

8

laughed outright, barely able to catch her breath. If there were any witnesses to the last ten minutes of her eventful evening, they'd be rolling on the floor laughing.

She turned her head slightly to see Jada sitting against the vanity, wiping her eyes and laughing too. Her expensive dress hiked up and barely covering her most precious gift, looked as if it had been trampled. Toni knew that if her cousin had a clue of how disheveled her hair was, she would be out for blood.

"How is it that I always get roped into messes like this whenever I'm anywhere near you?" Jada rested her head against the wall. "Please. Tell me why this always happens."

Still on her knees, Toni rested her forehead against the coolness of the tub not caring how crazy she probably looked. All she needed was a couple of minutes to regroup. "It doesn't *always* happen. Besides, you should be thanking me that I bring excitement and variety to your life."

"Girl, please. I have enough excitement and variety in my life. It's you who needs to get her act together and stop dating these jerks. I think MJ was right the other night. At some point you need to ask yourself, 'When am I going to stop dating these losers?'"

Toni lifted her head and glared at her cousin. "Not all of my dates are losers, and I don't appreciate you two talking about me behind my back. I'm sure there are more interesting subjects to discuss than my social life." Granted some of her choices in men as of late were questionable, but that was nobody's business but hers. "And another thing, how is MJ going to talk about who anyone dates when all she does is stomp on the pride of every man she comes in contact with and treat them like crap?"

Toni loved all of her cousins, but Martina (MJ) Jenkins lack of tact and straight-talk-no-chaser attitude was enough to make you want to slug her sometime. Five years older than Toni, Martina made it a point to try to school them all on why men were the lowest form of human life and how they were only good for sex and at times, according to Martina, weren't that good at that.

"Hey don't get mad at us because you keep picking boneheads." She waved a hand in Ronald's direction. "It's not like you can't do better. You're smart, have a good job, and you're cute – but not as cute as me," she flipped her dark hair over her shoulder, then glanced down at her dress and adjusted the thin shoulder straps. "Girl, you're a Jenkins. A proud, educated black woman who can do anything you set your mind to do. You might as well face it. Ever since you broke up with cutie-pie Craig Logan, you have been scraping the bottom of the barrel for male companionship. Your drunk boyfriend is proof. You can continue to be in denial if you want, but until you get yourself together, we're going to keep talking about you."

"What?" Toni turned slightly, still gripping the edge of the tub. "What are you talking about? I'm not in denial about anything. I have not—"

"Ahem."

All talk ceased. Toni was almost afraid to look back to see who had cleared their throat. There were two people she didn't want to see when she turned around - her grandfather or her pain-in-the butt cousin, MJ. Either one of them would make her feel worse than she already did about bringing Ronald to the party. *I knew I should have closed that damn door.*

Blowing out a frustrated breath she slowly turned her head toward the door and the steady thump of her heart went haywire. Heat soared to every cell in her body when her gaze met clear, hazel eyes that twinkled with mirth and belonged to the tall, gorgeous specimen whose broad shoulders were almost as wide as the bathroom doorway. *Craig.*

"Please tell me that guy isn't dead and that I don't have to arrest you two for murder."

CHAPTER TWO

"Well, well, well, if it isn't Cincinnati's *finest* and I mean that in every sense of the word." Jada stood and ran a manicured hand down the front of her black slip dress, smoothing out the wrinkles. She glanced at the wide mirror over the sink and turned her head back and forth before shaking her hair wildly. Craig almost laughed when she rubbed her lips together, smiled at her reflection, and struck a pose before turning to him. "Glad to see you, *Officer Logan*. I trust you can take it from here," she said on her way out of the oversized bathroom.

With an amused grin, Craig shook his head and watched her stroll down the hall as if she didn't have a care in the world. He got along well with all of Toni's family, but Jada, known for her oversized ego and theatrics, always cracked him up. He turned back to Toni and the smile slipped from his lips as she scurried to her feet, dusted off her knees and adjusted her drool-worthy red dress. A ripple of desire surged through his body and catapulted straight to his groin the moment their gazes collided. He'd worked a twelve-hour shift and was dog-tired when he first pulled up to the Jenkins' estate, but exhaustion no longer plagued him. Instead, his need to pull Toni into his arms and hold her close took root. Despite what he told himself when deciding on whether to attend her grandfather's birthday celebration, there was no way he'd be able to walk away from her tonight - at least not without tasting her tempting lips.

His heart pounded loudly in his ears as his gaze traveled from her perfectly made up face down her curvaceous body and shapely legs until his perusal stopped at her red strappy shoes. The eight months of them being apart suddenly felt like eight years as he slowly took her all in, realizing just how much he had missed her. *God she's beautiful.* So many days had come and gone when he wanted to call her, or just see her for a minute, but he'd kept his word. When she walked away from their relationship, she made him promise not to seek her out, telling him that she needed space. After seeing her tonight, all bets were off. No way could he be in her presence and not want what they once had.

"What are you doing here?" she asked, her sexy voice but a whisper.

When he didn't speak right away, she nervously pushed a lock of her long, thick hair behind her ear and peeked at the big brute lying at her feet. Glancing down at him, Craig wondered what she was thinking. Was she seriously dating this guy?

"Peyton invited me," Craig finally answered.

He leaned against the doorjamb and tucked his hands into his pants pockets. Eyes as warm as fresh-baked chocolate chip cookies on a cold winter's day stared back at him, and he shifted his stance to hide the evidence of his sudden arousal. He wasn't surprised by the ardent effect she still had on him, but right now wasn't the best time to indulge in what his body craved from her.

She glanced away. Her gaze bounced from him to the jerk on the floor and then back to him again. Why was she nervous? Toni was one of the most confident women he'd ever met, and right now her behavior didn't fit her usual self-assured personality. If anything, watching her actions now reminded him of a time, early in their relationship, when she was slow to let down her guard and unwilling to share her desires, needs, and even her fears.

"So what's going on?" He nodded at the man on the floor. "I assume he's alive."

Her mouth dropped open and her hands flew to her hips as she narrowed her eyes at Craig.

"Of course he's alive. He just had a little too much to drink."

"A little? Hell, the guy is passed out on your grandparent's bathroom floor. I'd say he's way past drunk." At that moment, her inebriated friend groaned and rolled to his side.

"Oh, thank goodness." Toni fell to her knees, pushed him onto his back and patted his cheek. "Ronald, wake up. Come on, we have to get you out of here. I need you to wake up."

Craig straightened and his body tensed. With a good view of her shapely butt as she leaned over her date, he couldn't stop himself from zoning in on her smooth toned legs and dainty feet. He had always been a leg-man, but when it came to Toni, he loved everything about her, from her curvy, petite body to her smart mouth. And right now, her mouth was a little too close to this guy's face.

"Come on, Ronald, wake up." She shook his shoulders, but when that didn't work, she went back to patting his cheek.

It wasn't so much that she was touching this Ronald guy in an intimate way that bothered Craig. The fact that she had her hands on another man period sent his jealous meter into overdrive.

"Maybe you need to slap him a little harder," Craig said, still standing near the doorway. "Or better yet, I'd be happy to do the honors." He moved forward and burst out laughing when she glared at him over her shoulder.

"Better yet, maybe I should slap you for just standing there and not offering to help me get him up and out of here!"

Craig chuckled, glad to see the fire within her hadn't burned out. Now this was the Toni he loved and missed.

"And why would I do that? He's *your* date." He snapped his fingers. "As a matter of fact, I should really get to the party, maybe grab something to eat, dance a little and get *my* drink on."

He turned and walked back to the door.

"Yikes!" Toni yelped. "Ronald, let me go."

Craig glanced back to see that Ronald had palmed Toni's butt and had pulled her on top of him.

"Ju … just lay heeere with me, baby," he mumbled, his eyes still closed. "Ne … need sleep ri … right now. Big da … daddy will gi … give you some lovin—"

"Ah, hell no!" With one long step, Craig reached for Toni's elbow and pulled her to her feet. His first thought was to plant his size twelve on top of her date's chest, but thinking that probably wouldn't be the best idea, he lifted Ronald by the front of his shirt. "Get your ass up," he growled.

"Be careful, Craig! You're going to hurt him."

Craig slammed him against the wall. "Oh, please, it's not as if he can feel anything." Craig wanted to knock him around for even being with Toni. The guy wasn't so drunk that he didn't know what he was doing when he planted his large hands on her butt.

Ronald slurred something unintelligible, and Craig held him tighter against the wall, turning his head when he got a whiff of his offensive breath. Why in the heck was he even holding his punk-ass up?

"Okay, since you have him standing, help me get him into the car." Toni straightened the rug that was in front of the tub and headed for the door.

"And then what?" Craig said through gritted teeth, not moving. "It's not as if you'll be able to get him out of the car and into his house. He's twice your size and sloppy drunk." The thought of Toni going anywhere with this man didn't sit right with him. Whether he was wasted or not there was no way Craig was allowing her to leave with him.

Craig stole a glance at Toni, her bottom lip clasped between her teeth as if trying to decide what to do.

"Maybe you can help me get him home." Her voice was as timid as a puppy walking into a new home.

Craig studied the woman before him. Her gorgeous brown eyes could make him do almost anything, but he refused to let her off that easy. "And why would I do that?"

She stepped to him and jabbed her finger into his bicep. "Doesn't this fall under your job duties as a police officer? Didn't you vow to serve and protect?"

"I'm off duty," he cracked. "So any serving and protecting is at my will and right now I don't feel like helping you sneak this jerk away from your grandfather's party. Besides, what would Mr. Jenkins think about your leaving his celebration so early? It's not every day a man turns seventy-five."

"Aw, come on Craig." She stomped her foot like a two-year-old and grabbed hold of his arm but quickly pulled her hands away, a glint of surprise in her eyes. She stepped back, and he suspected she felt the same spark of desire he felt, but she quickly recovered. "I need you. I mean I need your help. Please do this for me."

Craig could never deny her anything, even when her request involved helping her handle some low-life who clearly wasn't worth her efforts, but there was no way he wasn't going to get something out of this.

"I'll help you on one condition. Have dinner with me."

***

Toni leaned back and narrowed her eyes. "What?"

"You heard me." Craig readjusted Ronald against the wall, ignoring her date's mumbling. "If you want me to help you get this bum home - to his house," he emphasized, "then you have to agree to have dinner with me Friday night."

Toni hesitated. Intense hazel eyes sprinkled with specks of green and laced with a light brown stared at her, awaiting her response. She would love to have dinner with him, heck, she'd love to spend the rest of her life with him, but there lay the problem. Craig already had the big house and the white picket fence, but he wanted the wife and the three-point-five kids to complete the fairytale. The problem in a nutshell was that he wanted her to be a part of that dream, and she couldn't give him what he wanted.

17

"I can't believe you." She glanced back at the bathroom door and then closed it. Returning her attention to Craig she said, "After all we've been through, has it really come to this? You're going to blackmail me into having dinner with you?"

"Hey, if it means spending time with you, I'm not ashamed to do whatever I have to do. Besides, I don't see it as blackmail. I see my request as being nothing more than a man, who is still in love with you, asking you out to dinner." He shrugged. "But you can call my invitation whatever you want. I do know one thing though. If you don't make up your mind in the next five seconds, your drunk boyfriend here is going to find his ass back on the cold marble tile. So what's it going to be, Sweetheart?"

Toni scrunched up her face and twisted her lips into a frown. Could she have dinner with Craig and then just walk away? Walk away from the only man she's ever loved? Walk away from a man who had the ability to make her heart rate triple and her body sizzle with just a look. Heck, occupying the same space with him now, his hot sexy body only inches from her and his unfaltering gaze appearing to look right through her was almost more than she could handle. How in the world would she be able to break bread with him and not want to jump his bones?

She glanced at Ronald. She knew Craig well enough to know that if she said no, Ronald would hit the floor quicker than a hooker's panties and Toni would be right back where she started. She wouldn't be able to hide out in the bathroom for much longer, and the last thing she wanted was for her grandfather to get a hold of Ronald, or her for that matter. *God! Why me?*

She finally threw up her hands. "Oh, all right. I'll go out to dinner with you Friday, but I'm not going to enjoy myself!"

CHAPTER THREE

Toni snuggled deeper into the passenger seat of Craig's BMW 428i, the soft leather wrapped around her like a silk cocoon on a cold winter's night. She needed a new vehicle. The smooth ride of Craig's car made her realize just how bad her own truck drove.

They headed back to her grandparent's estate, neither of them saying much since dropping Ronald off at his house. It took everything she had not to steal another glance at Craig's profile. She still couldn't believe she was sitting next to him. Eight months was a long time to go without being able to stare into those sexy eyes that had unlocked her heart and soul a year and a half ago. Everything about him screamed hot dreamy hunk and the sheer essence of the man he was on the inside made him that much hotter.

Realization dawned on her. If she could barely sit next to him in a car without wanting to leap onto his lap and have buck-wild sex with him, how the heck was she going to be able to have dinner with him and not fall back into his arms?

"What in the hell were you doing with that jerk?" Craig glanced at her and then back at the road, gripping the steering wheel tight enough for Toni to notice the rippling muscles on his forearm. "Anyone who would get drunk while at an event with his woman's family is clearly not someone you want to be hanging out with."

Toni's pulse sped up and she gritted her teeth. All thoughts of having sex with him flew out the window and were replaced with thoughts of ringing his neck.

"It's bad enough I have to put up with dating speeches from my cousins," she said, her voice getting louder with each word. "There is no way I'm going to sit here and take dating advice from you."

"I'm not trying to tell you what to do. I just think you can do better. As a matter of fact, you have done better." He jutted out his chin. The smug look on his face was like that of a hawk feasting on its latest conquest.

"What are you trying to say? That I'm not capable of choosing a decent date? That no one can compare to you? So what, you think you're the only man worthy of spending time with me and my family?"

He glanced at her again and frowned. "Well...yeah. Compared to that chump, Ronald, I'm frickin Prince Charming."

"Whatever." Toni waved his comment off and huffed. She folded her arms across her chest and ran her hands up and down her bare arms. In her haste to leave the party, she'd left without her shawl. The temperature had plummeted into the forties, and it was hard to believe it was springtime.

Craig shot her a look, his eyes zoned in on her hands moving up and down her arms. He reached over and turned up the heat, grabbed his suit jacket from the back seat and handed it to her.

"Listen, I don't want to argue with you. My only concern is your safety, and I don't think going out with a guy like Ronald is a good idea."

Character is built by the choices we make. The words that had been playing around in Toni's head all evening traveled to the forefront of her mind as she stared out the passenger side window. She blew out a breath and dropped her head against the headrest. What was wrong with her? She wasn't some little hoochie who had to settle for any man that came along. Successful, handsome men approached her all the time. So why was she dating losers?

She knew why. It started with trying to fix the hole in her heart and then it was more about choosing guys who were just out to have a good time, not those who wanted to get serious and settle down, like Craig.

"So," Craig cleared his throat, "have you been dating this Ronald guy long?"

Toni could tell he tried to sound casual, but his voice was tense, almost strangled. His expression was anything but casual.

"No," she said absently. "We weren't dating. I've gone out with him a couple of times, but nothing serious." Closing her eyes, she fell back into what they once had—seamless conversation.

Seconds later, her eyes popped opened. Hold up, why was she answering his questions? He no longer had a right to question what she did, or whom she dated even if a small part of her wanted him to know.

"So I guess that means you're not seeing anyone seriously." Craig's voice held a hint of uncertainty, so unlike his take charge personality.

"I guess it does." She turned her back to him and fully faced the passenger window as he arrived on her grandparents' street. It was time to put an end to the direction that the conversation was going. The last thing she wanted was for Craig to think there was a chance for them to get back together.

Toni shrugged off his jacket and returned it to the back seat with every intention of thanking him and then jumping out of the car, but then he touched her. A jolt of adrenaline whipped through her body and her heart rate kicked into double time. *Damn this man.* The hold he had on her arm was gentle, yet firm. She stared down at his hand and then turned to face him.

Those eyes. Eyes so beautifully intense reached down to the depths of her soul, and all the love she once felt for him came rushing back. *Double damn him.*

"Toni." He swept a lock of her hair off her face and the back of his hand slid down her cheek. She leaned into his touch and her eyes fluttered closed. "I love you," he said. "I know you don't want to hear that, but I do. That means I care about your safety and baby I know guys like Ronald. They're bad news." Toni heard concern in his voice, but his words of love caressed her like a gentle summer breeze against her heated skin.

She risked a glance at him and the heart-rending tenderness of his gaze touched her from the top of her head to the soles of her feet. "I know." She didn't bother clarifying which statement she was agreeing to because both statements were true – Craig loved her and Ronald was bad news.

"I'll walk you to the door."

He strolled around to the passenger side of the car and opened her door, extending his hand to help her out of the vehicle. As they approached the house, his large hand settled comfortably around her smaller one while they walked around to the back entrance.

Toni nodded to a few people leaving out of the front entrance, not recognizing any of them. But the bass of the music bumped loud enough to be heard outside and it was safe to say the party was still going strong. When they neared the door, Craig squeezed her hand and stopped short.

"I think I'll say goodnight here."

Toni glanced down at their joined hands. How could something that felt so right be so wrong? She'd be the first to admit that they were perfect together, in every way, except they wanted two different things. He wanted to have a family, and she couldn't give him that.

She eased her hand from his grip. "Craig, thanks for everything tonight. I know you didn't have to help me with Ronald, but I appreciate that you did."

He shrugged. "I would say, no problem call me anytime you need help with one of your boyfriends, but I wouldn't mean it. Actually, if I ever come face to face with another one of your *dates*, I'll probably smash his face in." His cocky tone sent a dizzying current racing through her. Or maybe it was the way his tempting mouth spat out the fighting words that made her pulse thump loudly in her ears.

"You know since you're here," Toni glanced up at the house and then back at him, "maybe you should um, come in. Have something to eat and get something to drink ... if you want."

Without warning, he stepped forward and crushed his mouth over hers, a sexual stirring Toni hadn't felt in months shot through her body like a tactical missile hurling toward its target. It was as if her arms had a mind of their own when they wrapped around his neck. Craig was never one for holding back on what he wanted, making it clear where he stood on a subject or a situation, and the passion behind this kiss left no doubt to what he wanted. And damn if she didn't want it too.

The fierce pounding of her heart grew louder when he slipped his arm around her waist, drawing her closer, his tongue tangling with hers. She couldn't pull away even if she wanted to. Their tongues danced to a familiar beat and a throaty moan slipped through her lips. God she had missed him. His spicy citrus scent and the gentleness of his kiss lured her in like a butterfly to a Marigold plant, reminding her of what she'd been missing. The voice of reason urged her to stop and get as far away from him as possible, but his kiss touched a longing inside her that brought back memories of their passionate lovemaking sessions. Sessions that lasted hours upon hours and left her exhausted, yet satisfied. No man had ever made her feel as desired and cherished as Craig and she doubted anyone ever would.

His hand traveled up her spine and stopped at the base of her neck where he gently pulled her even closer, his fingers lost in the thickness of her hair. This is what she needed, what she craved. Craig's husky groan filled the air when he backed her up against the brick of the house. As his tongue continued to explore the inner recesses of her mouth, his erection pressed against her stomach.

"Do you feel the effect you still have on me?" The roughness of his tone a sure sign he was reaching the point of no return.

"Mmm hmm. It's the same effect you're having on me," she said breathlessly, her own control teetering on the edge.

He released her lips and her body protested until he lowered his head to her neck. The scorching kisses stoked the flame he had already started within her, and she gripped his shoulders unable to keep her lower body from grinding against him. Her mind screamed stop, but the moisture pooling between her thighs made her yearn for more. She grabbed a fist full of his shirt and pulled him back to her lips, missing the sweetness of his mouth against hers. The physical attraction was staggering; he still had the power to make her body come alive with just a kiss.

"Really, TJ? Out here?"

As if a tub of ice water were dumped on top of her head, an involuntary shiver gripped Toni's body and her eyes flew open. *Oh crap.* She pushed against Craig's hard chest and slipped from his grasp. Her breath came in short spurts as she yanked down the hem of her dress that had mysteriously risen to just below her butt during their tongue aerobics. Though they were at least a foot apart, she felt as if Craig's hands still caressed her body. Her cheeks heated at the thought of how far they almost went. How could she have gotten so caught up? All she needed was for one of her grandparents to catch her making out against their house while they entertained some of the state's most important dignitaries.

She stole a glance at her cousin Kevin, Jada's brother, who had interrupted them and was confused by the huge grin that broke out on his face.

"Ah man, Craig? Dude, I didn't know that was you." Kevin gave him a one-arm hug, slapping him on the back. "Man, where in the heck have you been? I thought you were one of TJ's … uh … I mean … uh … are you two back together?"

"No," Toni responded quickly, her hand against her chest still unable to bring her racing heart under control. "Craig helped me take care of something."

"Yeah, just helped her *dump* some trash." Craig's sex charged voice and the raw desire she saw in his eyes reignited the flames in her body. She clearly had a problem when the man could just look at her and make her panties wetter. She shifted uncomfortably under the intensity of his stare and glanced away.

"Kevin?" A woman's strained voice called from in front of the house.

"I'll be right there," her cousin yelled. "All right, Craig, it was good seeing you man. We'll have to hook up and shoot some pool when you're free."

"You know how to reach me."

They did the whole brother-man hug thing and Toni wondered just how many members of her family Craig maintained contact with after they broke up.

"Oh, and Toni, uncle Joe and your mom said they want to see you before you leave tonight and Grampa's looking for you," Kevin said over his shoulder. "Something about you explaining to him what happen to Gram's plant." He laughed as he walked away. Toni didn't know which conversation would be worse, the one with her parents or the one with her grandfather.

"Now where were we?" Craig's arms snaked around her waist and he would have planted a kiss on her lips had she not punched him in the shoulder.

"What?" He jerked back. His hand instinctively went to the offended appendage, though he probably barely felt the punch.

"You know what!" She said through gritted teeth. "What the heck was that all about?"

Craig threw up his hands and shrug. "What? Kevin and I shoot pool sometime and—"

"Not that. I'm talking about that kiss."

A slow grin slid across his lips. "That was about me tasting you again. And I must say, you taste even sweeter than I remember."

He stepped toward her and she took a giant step back, her palms held out in front of her.

"Craig, listen. I appreciate your help this evening, but I hope you don't think that kiss meant anything. I'll go to dinner with you Friday, but that's all. You and I are friends. We can never be more than that."

"Yeah, you keep telling yourself that, but that kiss says we are a lot more than just friends." He moved forward and cupped her chin, his lips only inches from hers. "I let you go once and it was the biggest mistake I ever made. Now that I've tasted you, I am going to work like hell to make you mine again." He lowered his head and his mouth came down over hers. The sweet caress of his soft lips against hers pulled her into submission. She could feel the protective shield she'd carefully erected over her heart melt away. "And that's a promise," he said when he lifted his head. "Come on, let's go inside. I'm suddenly a little hungry."

***

The sexy sway of Toni's hips as she made her way toward the bathroom lured Craig's attention away from the toast given on behalf of Steven Jenkins. Craig couldn't get enough of Toni. He knew the moment he kissed her lips that he'd want more, but so far he hadn't had another opportunity, which was probably a good thing. She was the most stubborn woman he knew and she was holding on tight to the idea that they were just friends. Or at least that's what she'd been telling the family members who were bold enough to ask if they had gotten back together. She quickly told them no, but little did she know he had other plans.

A huge round of applause drew Craig's attention back to the front of the ballroom, where the family had set up a Plexiglas podium for those who wanted to say something about the patriarch of the Jenkins family.

"Finally, I get to speak." Steven Jenkins laughed when he strolled to the front of the room, the base of his voice as robust as the man himself. At over six-feet tall, with mostly gray hair, skin the color of sandalwood and a football linebackers build, Steven Jenkins didn't look a day over fifty. It was clear by the admiration on the faces of the invited guest that he was well respected.

Craig spotted Toni the moment she re-entered the room and headed his way. Everything about her screamed sexy from her long flowing hair to her sensual strut. She might've been petite, but her aura shouted Amazon goddess.

"What did I miss?" she asked out of breath and accepted the glass of white wine from Craig.

"Not much, your grandfather just started his speech." Craig whispered close to her ear fighting his sudden arousal brought on by the delicate scent of her perfume and her nearness.

"Oh good. I tried to hurry. I knew the moment I stepped out of the room he would go to the podium."

"As most of you know, family is everything to me," Steven Jenkins said, leaning slightly against the podium, cool and confident. "I'm the proud father of seven children and fifteen wonderful grandchildren. But I can't believe I'm seventy-five. I don't feel a day over seventy-four." Everyone laughed with him. "Seriously, though, I am so blessed to stand before you this evening. I know you came here to celebrate my birthday with me, but there are five young women here tonight whom I want to raise my glass to."

Craig heard Toni groan next to him. "You okay?" he asked, his hand against her back. Touching her reminded him of how good she felt in his arms earlier. Kissing and holding her again was like coming home.

"I'm fine. He's known for long-winded speeches and he's good at embarrassing us. I'm hoping that he doesn't do either tonight."

Since Toni didn't step away, Craig kept his arm around her and enjoyed the feel of her body close to his.

"Will you all lift your glasses with me? Though I love all of my grandchildren the same, I'd like to make a special toast to my five beautiful granddaughters who made this celebration possible. Peyton, Martina, Toni, Christina and Jada, I don't see all of you right now," he scanned the crowd, "but I'm sure you're all here."

"We're here, Grampa," Jada yelled from the other side of the room.

"Good, because I want you all to know that I am so proud of you ladies. Not only do you all do a fine job of overseeing the family business, but thank you for this wonderful birthday celebration." He glanced around the room at his party guests. "I know my family, especially my grandchildren, get sick of my speeches about integrity, character, and family first, but it does me proud when they take heed of what I've said and have all grown up to be upstanding citizens." He paused when everyone clapped.

"Tonight someone asked me what I was most proud of. I'd have to say I'm most proud of my family. The Jenkins Clan, as many have referred to us over the years, is also my biggest accomplishment."

"Hey!" Toni's grandmother, Katherine Jenkins piped in. "You didn't raise them by yourself." Laughter flowed throughout the room and even more so when Steven Jenkins reached for his wife and she swatted playfully at his hand before joining him at the podium.

Craig had always admired the Jenkins family. The love they had for one another was evident whenever he was around them. And Steven Jenkins took his role as patriarch very seriously, making sure to always be there whenever his family needed him.

"They're something aren't they?" Toni leaned into him, tears of joy in her eyes.

"Yeah, they are." He rubbed his hand up and down her arm and kissed the top of her hair. "And so are you." She stiffened in his arm and glanced up at him.

"Craig." Her tone held a warning, but he ignored it. No matter what she said or thought, they were getting back together.

"Craig nothing, I'm just stating a fact." He held her gaze.

"Listen, I don't want you to get the wrong idea about you and me this evening." She pulled out of his grasp and he dropped his arm to his side. "I appreciate everything you did for me tonight and I'm really glad you came to the party, but this doesn't change a thing."

"Okay," is all he said. He returned his attention to the front of the room and sipped from his glass of scotch, undeterred by her words. Surely, she knew that when his lips touched hers earlier, she became his again. A gust of determination flowed through him and he was more intent than ever to put an end to their separation. He didn't know what it would take, but Toni would be his wife before the end of the year.

"Please raise your glasses with me again," Steven Jenkins said and wrapped his free arm around his wife's shoulder and placed a kiss against her temple. He returned his attention to his guests. "On my birthday, I celebrate family. Here's to family loyalty and love that grows deeper with every breath we take."

I'll drink to that. Craig sipped from his glass and noticed Toni had taken a timid sip from hers. Exhilaration pumped through his veins at the thought of them reuniting. She didn't know it yet, but the two of them together again … was only a matter of time.

CHAPTER FOUR

"Now you know you can't come in here unless you have my nephew with you," Craig said when he opened his front door.

"Don't you see my hands are full?" His brother, Derek, countered. "So open the damn door and quit playin'."

Craig laughed and stepped back to let his brother into the house, grabbing one of the suitcases that dangled from his hand. "Seriously though, where's li'l man? And why does it look like you're moving in for weeks instead of just a few days?"

"Jason's at daycare." Derek headed for the stairs, already knowing which room he would claim during his stay. "And I have all of this junk because your nephew insisted on bringing tons of movies for you and him to watch, as well as every toy he owns." Once he stepped into the bedroom he dropped the bags onto the bench at the foot of the bed. "Oh, and I almost strangled that kid this morning." He turned to Craig and accepted the suitcase that he'd carried. "He pitched a fit when I took him to daycare, thanks to you."

"What? What did I do?"

"He claimed he couldn't go to daycare today because you were waiting for him. I *literally* had to carry that boy into the center, kicking and screaming."

Craig threw his head back and laughed. He always enjoyed his brother's stories about Jason, who was smarter than most three-year-olds. As a single parent, Derek had proved without a doubt that fathers could raise kids on their own, providing their child with a nurturing and loving environment despite it not being a two-parent home. After one year of marriage, Derek divorced his wife, fought for custody of their only son and won. Craig couldn't see the outcome going any other way and nor could the judge once he considered Derek's ex-wife had abandoned him, and their son when Jason was six months old. She claimed that marriage and raising kids were too much work.

Craig didn't care how much work marriage and parenting took, he wanted a family and he wanted that family with Toni. He had always pictured himself married with kids by the time he was thirty. He missed that goal by a year, but this year that marriage goal would be a reality.

"Hey, holler if you need anything," Craig said from the bedroom doorway. "I'll be downstairs making breakfast."

"I'm right behind you."

"So how's business?" Craig pulled eggs, onions, mushrooms and tomatoes from the refrigerator and placed them on the center island.

"Not bad. I just signed a nice contract with Lexington Technology. I'm drawing up the plans for a remodel of the second and third floors of their downtown location."

"Ah, man, that's cool." They shared a fist bump and Craig pulled a pack of bacon out of the refrigerator. "I guess becoming a freelance architect is paying off. That's your third big project this year."

"Yeah, I know. It's working out a lot better than I expected." He grabbed a couple of mugs from the cabinet near the sink and poured a cup of coffee for him and Craig. "But enough about me how was Steven Jenkins' birthday party Saturday? Did you see Toni?"

"I did." He told his brother about Ronald, and how he found him held up in the bathroom with Toni and Jada looming over him. Craig had to laugh himself when he recalled the look on Toni's face when he showed up.

Derek shook his head. "Toni never ceases to amaze me with the crazy stuff she gets caught up in and to have both her and Jada dragging this guy around the house. I would have paid money to see that." He sipped his black coffee. "Both of them together probably don't weigh as much as that guy, yet they were able to get him to the bathroom."

"I know, man. That goes to show you can't judge them by their looks." Craig placed an omelet in front of his brother. "You think Jason keeps you on your toes, I feel the same way about Toni. I never told you half the stuff she roped me into when we were dating."

"You two are actually perfect for each other, a good balance. You can provide her with stability and keep her out of trouble. She can add some fun to your life, loosen you up a little."

Craig held his coffee mug between his hands and stared into the dark liquid. "Yeah, we are perfect for each other."

His thoughts veered sharply to the memory of his lips touching her soft ones. He intended to give her a quick kiss goodbye, but that well-intended friendly kiss quickly spiraled into a lip-lock session that he would remember for days to come. Craig couldn't explain the powerful hold she had on him. All he knew was that he wanted her back.

Before Cynthia was killed, they had dated for three years and at the time of her death, they were engaged. But not once did he remember his pulse racing whenever she was within five feet of him. Or his throat going dry whenever he saw her in a sexy outfit. And never had he wanted to make love to her so badly that he was willing to forgo all common sense and take her up against a brick house. Which is exactly what he would've done to Toni had her cousin not interrupted.

He blew out a breath and removed his sweaty palms from around his coffee mug before he swiped them down his pant legs. He could still feel her against his body, taste her sweet lips. Craig sat back in his seat. He inhaled deeply and then exhaled deeply a few times until his heart rate returned to normal.

"So," his brother strung out the word, studying him as if he knew where Craig's thoughts were for the past few minutes. "Did you get a chance to talk to Toni about getting back together?"

Craig cleared his throat and leaned forward, his elbows planted firmly on the table. "Well, she knows my feelings for her haven't changed, yet she's still fighting the thought of us being together." He traced the curve of the handle of the oversized coffee mug. "But I'm going to work like crazy to prove to her that we're a perfect fit and that I'm not going anywhere."

His brother grinned. "And how are you going to do that, especially since you're technically still a cop?"

"I'm a detective and that's different than being a cop. Besides, my gut tells me that although she used my being a cop as an excuse to break up there's something else keeping her from me. I just have to figure out what that something is."

"Well," Derek lifted his coffee mug for a toast, "I hope you two can find your way back to each other. She'd make a perfect sister-in-law."

They tapped their mugs together. "I agree."

***

Toni pulled into Jenkins & Sons Construction parking lot in no mood to do anything. Her two days off were a welcome break but didn't erase the memories of the weekend. Her anticipated fun and relaxing long weekend was anything but after dealing with Ronald and Craig Saturday night. If that were not bad enough, she'd been dodging Ronald's phone calls since Sunday morning, not knowing how else to tell him that she wasn't interested in seeing him anymore.

MJ might've been right. Men are more trouble than they're worth.

Memories of Craig came to mind as she climbed out of her truck. She grabbed her clipboard and headed into the building. Toni might've been surprised to see him standing in the doorway of her grandparents' bathroom, but what didn't surprise her was how her body responded to him even before he kissed her. The sexual pull between them was as strong as she remembered.

"Morning, TJ," the receptionist greeted when Toni walked into the front desk area. A large counter with two desks behind it took up a small portion of the area that was flooded by sunlight from the picture windows at the front of the building.

"Morning, Tam."

Tammy was one of few Jenkins & Sons Construction employees who weren't family, but their grandfather had a policy. If you worked for the company, that made you family.

"Looks like the painters finally finished," Toni said pointing at the wall behind Tammy where the company's logo, a giant scripted J & S with the words Jenkins & Sons Construction below the letters were painted. "The design came out really nice. I like that they used the red to outline the black 3-D letters. The extra detail definitely makes them pop."

"I agree. Your cousin Christina finished painting about an hour ago. Oh and you had a delivery this morning." She stood from her chair and carried over a large vase of flowers that sat on the desk near the rear of the reception area. "There's a card." She pointed and wiggled her eyebrows.

Toni grinned and accepted the vase of roses, gerberas and lilies. "These are beautiful," she said and plucked the card from its holder.

I'm looking forward to Friday night, Craig.

She held the card to her chest and a small smile touched her lips. A nervous flutter settled in her stomach when she inhaled the faint fragrance and touched one of the delicate petals. Craig sent her flowers at least once a month while they were dating, and Toni didn't realize how much she missed the gesture until now.

She took one last whiff of the beautiful flower arrangement and then placed the glass vase on the end of the counter for the office staff and visitors to enjoy.

"Also, you just had a phone call. Actually, you've had a few." Tammy handed Toni several yellow slips of paper.

"Thanks. Is Peyton in yet?"

"Yep," Tammy said as the telephone started ringing. "She's in her office, but I think she's meeting with Jerry."

Toni headed toward the stairs. She sifted through her messages as she walked, but stopped short when she read the last two. She didn't have to ask how Ronald got her work number. What she couldn't understand was how a grown, successful, Boris Kodjoe lookalike couldn't move on and leave her the hell alone. Surely there were plenty of women interested in getting with him. Why was he still calling her? It was one thing to blow up her cell phone, but another to contact her at work. *This has to stop.*

She glanced at her watch and trotted up the stairs toward Peyton's office. Toni was behind schedule and needed to get more information on the lateral pipe job that she wasn't looking forward to repairing. As far as she was concerned, all in-ground work was a pain and this was one job she wished she had the option of handing off to someone else.

Hearing raised voices Toni slowed when she reached the top of the landing. Suddenly the idea of speaking with Peyton didn't seem as appealing, especially once Peyton finished with her brother. She was one of the most laid-back people she knew, but her cousin took running the family business very serious and lately Jerry seemed to be on a mission to sabotage everything he touched.

Peyton's brother, despite being one of the smartest men Toni knew, was also one of the laziest people she knew.

"What is wrong with you?" Toni heard Peyton through her closed office door. "You're twenty-three years old and still act like you're five! You say I don't respect you, but let me tell you something respect has to be earned. If you don't get your shit together, you'll be looking for another job."

Toni plopped down on the leather sofa outside Peyton's door, trying not to listen to their conversation, but finding it hard not to eavesdrop considering Peyton was yelling, which was unusual. Toni knew how hard it was for her to reprimand her brother, not because he was family, but because they were so close. When everyone else had given up on him, Peyton was the one who said to give him time, or that he was still trying to find his place in life. But now he had found a way to alienate the one person who had always had his back.

Toni heard Jerry mumble something shortly before the door flew open and he stepped into the hall. He glanced at her and nodded, but kept walking without tossing out one of his usual wisecracks.

"Is it safe to come in?" Toni asked, standing at Peyton's doorway. She glanced around the dimly lit office with its large clunky furniture leftover from when her grandfather ran the company and wasn't surprised to see that the blinds, covering the wall of windows, were all closed. The only light emitted in the space was from the floor lamp across the room and the small lamp on the corner of Peyton's desk. She claimed she did her best work in the dark, which was funny seeing that she was an electrician.

"Yeah," Peyton said just above a whisper from behind her desk, her head resting in her hands. "I give up. I don't know what to do with him."

"Well, you said yourself you can't help someone who doesn't want to be helped."

"I know ... but he is too smart to let all that knowledge go to waste." She dropped her hands and shook her head. "I had high hopes for him, but now I'm not so sure."

"I heard he's been skipping out of apprentice classes. Maybe being an electrician is not what he really wants."

"Then he needs to tell me. It's not as if he were forced into the construction trades. Like the rest of us, he had a choice." She stood and carried a folder to a file cabinet a few feet from her desk. "I only hope he gets his act together before he gets into major trouble. You know what they say about idle minds."

"Yeah, I know."

"All right, enough about Jerry. What's going on with you?" She slammed the file cabinet drawer closed. "I saw Craig at the party Saturday."

Toni studied her cousin. "Why didn't you tell me you'd invited him?"

Peyton shrugged and returned to her seat. "Didn't think about it." She shuffled papers around on her desk and Toni was almost sure her cousin intentionally didn't tell her.

"I also heard you had an adventurous evening while the rest of us were mingling with Grampa's guests. How did you talk your *ex*-boyfriend into helping you get your *new* boyfriend out of the house? And rumor has it that you were caught in a serious lip-lock with your ex that left you panting so hard you couldn't see straight."

Toni's face heated. An image of Craig and their kiss came to mind, and she shifted in her seat. Before Saturday, she had finally reached the point of not thinking about him every second of every day, and now she couldn't stop thinking about him. Couldn't stop thinking about his lips against hers, his strong hard body rubbed up against her, making her feel passion she hadn't felt since the last time they were together.

"Seeing you stare off into space makes me think it must've been some kiss. Does this mean you two are going to try to work things out?"

Toni shook her head. "I already told you, Craig and I don't have a future together."

For years, she had avoided emotional attachments, but then Craig came along and she made the mistake of letting her guard down. Within forty-eight hours of meeting him, they had established a connection. She shared things with him she hadn't shared with those closest to her, but there were still some things he didn't know, things she'd never be able to share.

Toni's cell phone rang, interrupting their conversation. She pulled the intrusive device from the holster on her belt and glanced at the screen, groaning when she saw Ronald's phone number again. It made no sense that he was calling her. She shoved the phone back into the holster.

"Toni, you owe it to yourself to see if there is still something between you and Craig." Peyton's hand shot up when Toni opened her mouth to speak. "And don't you dare say you broke up with him because of his job." The authoritative tone Peyton used with her brother moments ago rang out. "I'm not buying that excuse. You dated him for over a year and then moved in with him. All the while you knew what he did for a living."

"Have you forgotten that he was almost killed?" Toni spat out and bolted from her chair. Pacing the room, she wondered why she was even having this conversation.

"But he wasn't killed Toni. He's very much alive. I know you took the death of his partner hard, thinking that it could have easily been Craig but–"

"Stop!" She pounded on the top of the file cabinet and whirled on her cousin. "Do you have any idea what it feels like to get a call, in the middle of the night, telling you that the man you love more than you love yourself has been shot and is in the hospital?" Her anger mounted with each word spoken.

Peyton shook her head.

"I didn't think so!" Toni rubbed her forehead knowing that she needed to calm down, but finding it hard to reign in the explosion of anxiety bouncing around in her gut. "It didn't matter that he wasn't seriously hurt. He was laid up in a hospital bed with blood stained clothes, and the sight of that blood scared me to death. I can't put myself through that again."

"I think you're afraid."

"You're damn right I'm afraid. Whenever I think about the type of calls he responds to on any given night, it turns my blood to ice knowing that he could be killed by some lunatic."

"No, that's not what I'm talking about. You're afraid of something else. There is something else keeping you away from Craig. Even fear of him dying in the line of duty wouldn't make you run the way you did. It was at least a month after that incident that you walked away from him."

"PJ," Toni's warning tone drew a line in the sand and dared PJ to enter into dangerous territory.

"After the shooting, not once did you give any sign that you were going to leave him because of his job. Within a couple of weeks, you weren't even talking about the incident. What happened to make you walk away from the man you claimed was your soul mate?"

"I didn't *claim* he was my soul mate," she said before thinking and finished in a whisper, "he is my soul mate." She might've walked away, but what she felt for Craig she couldn't deny.

"Okay, then what happened to make you leave the man who has asked you to marry him more than once and told you that he wanted you to be the mother of his children? What happened to make you walk away from the man you loved, Toni?"

"PJ, please just leave it alone." Toni swallowed hard. The despair lodged in her throat threatened to choke her and she knew that if she didn't get herself together, she would say something that she'd have to take back later.

Toni swiped at the tears pooling in her eyes, her heart weighed heavy like an ant hauling a brick. She would never be able to tell Peyton or anyone else her real reason for leaving Craig. So many times she wanted to give him an honest explanation of why she couldn't marry him, but the words would never form. She could never drum up enough courage to share her deepest darkest secret knowing the disappointment she would see in his eyes when he found out why she turned down his marriage proposal.

She blew out a breath. "Cuz, I love you, and you have always had my back. I'll never be able to thank you for all you've done for me, but my relationship with Craig is no longer open for discussion." She snatched a Kleenex from the box on Peyton's desk and dropped back down in the chair she had vacated earlier. "We can either talk about the lateral pipe job," she dabbed at her eyes, "or we can go over the specs for the Duke Corporation project that's coming up, but I'm done talking about Craig and me."

Peyton studied her for a minute before saying, "Fine. I won't mention your relationship with Craig again." She opened an orange file folder that was sitting on her desk and passed a few documents to Toni. "Let's hold off on reviewing the specs for Duke until Wednesday. That's the work order for the lateral pipe job and a copy of the letter the client received from the city. Let me know if you have any questions. I told them that someone will be there …"

Toni half listened as her cousin rattled on about the job. God knows she missed Craig, but what could she do? His job might not have been her only reason for walking away from their relationship, but it still played a huge role in her decision. She would never forget the night that Derek, Craig's brother, called to tell her that Craig had been shot and was in the hospital asking for her. Shock, fear and a host of other emotions assaulted her all at once sending her into an overwhelming panic. Crying on the phone, she contacted Peyton who drove her to the hospital. Toni felt as if she had held her breath from the time she received the call until Craig wrapped her in his arms, assuring her that he was all right. The only other time in her life that fear had gripped her to the point of hysterics - the rape, and she never wanted to go through either experience ever again.

"Hopefully you'll be able to write up an estimate for the Smiths and get your assessment of the job to me by sometime tomorrow." Peyton's voice intruded on her thoughts. "The city is only giving them ten days to have the leak repaired before they begin to rack up substantial fines."

Toni wiped at her eyes again and took a deep breath. Standing, she held onto the back of the chair, more exhausted than she was when she first arrived. Thinking about the night Craig was shot was like reliving the terror all over again. The same emotions she felt back then caused an overwhelming desire to call him. But she wouldn't. She couldn't fall back into those old habits of checking in, especially not if she intended to maintain their "just friends" status.

"Okay, I'll make the Smiths my first stop and then head to Lorraine's Diner to see what's going on with their sump pump," Toni said, her voice sounding as shaky as she felt. "I'll probably finish the day over on 6th street to see how the guys are doing with the Cole's kitchen remodel."

"Sounds good." Her cousin studied her. "Are you going to be okay? I didn't mean to upset you."

Toni shrugged. "I'll be fine. It's just some days it's still hard."

Peyton nodded her understanding.

Toni's cell phone rang again when she stepped out of Peyton's office and this time the screen read *unknown*.

"Ronald, I told you to stop calling me! What part of not interested don't you understand?" Her tone was harsher than she intended, but right now she wasn't in the mood to deal with his nonsense.

Silence greeted her.

"Oh, so now you don't have anything to say? You've called five times in the last hour, say something! Just tell me - why are you still calling?"

"That's what I'd like to know." Craig's deep baritone voice held a hint of irritation edged with steel.

Toni stopped near the staircase and leaned against the wall. The last thing she needed was for Craig to get involved. Even with all the things she loved about him, he had his faults. Impatient, over protective, and at times possessive, but she knew, behind those faults, there was a good man who loved with all he had, hard and completely. Despite them no longer being together, she had no doubt he was still willing to fight her battles.

"When did the phone calls start, Toni?"

"Craig, let me handle this."

"I asked you a question," he said, his voice hard and unwavering. "If this asshole is harassing you, I want to know."

"I can handle him." She had already decided to get her cousin MJ to help teach Ronald a lesson if he didn't cease the calls. MJ's words alone could put fear in any man and would make him question whether or not he was really a man. "By the way, thank you for the flowers. They're absolutely gorgeous."

"You're welcome, but let's get back to this Ronald dude."

"Craig," Toni said exasperated that he wouldn't drop the subject, "I don't want you to get involved. You might do something you'll regret."

"The only thing I've ever regretted is letting you walk out of my life." Toni could picture him running his hand over his head, pacing the length of a room. "I doubt I'll regret anything I do to this guy."

"Craig, just stay away from him. Let me handle this my way and if I need you, I'll call you. Please, just stay away from him."

After a long silence he finally answered, "Fine, but that fool better hope I never run into him."

***

Craig tossed a paper coffee cup in the trash and sat back in his seat. Running his hand down his face and to his chin, he stroked the short hairs of his goatee. He couldn't stop thinking about the conversation he'd had with Toni earlier. She would kill him if she knew he had pulled up everything he could find on Ronald Kent, looking for anything that could justify him hunting the guy down. As far as he was concerned, Ronald calling her nonstop was enough of a reason for Craig to pay him a visit, but he wouldn't. He had promised Toni that he would let her handle the situation. One wrong move on Ronald's part though, and all deals were off.

"I'm quitting for real today."

Craig looked up and grinned. Floyd Hobson, his new partner as of six months ago, was as dedicated to his job as he was big and tall. Standing well over six feet and two hundred and fifty pounds, he didn't mince words and his bark was just as bad as his bite. After Julien, Craig's former partner was killed during a domestic violence call, Craig barely wanted to show up for work and definitely didn't want another partner, but then Floyd arrived. He'd transferred to Craig's precinct and they hit it off immediately.

"You do realize you say that every two weeks don't you?" He taunted Floyd.

"This time I mean it." He ran his hands through his short blond hair and then leaned on the desk facing Craig. "They just released Thomas James."

Craig's mouth flew open. "What?" The word caught in the tightness of his throat and came out like a croak. He gripped the edge of the desk and took several breaths before speaking again. "The guy all but confessed, how in the hell could they let him go?"

Floyd shrugged. "He got this big-time lawyer who says we didn't have enough evidence to hold him."

Craig stood and pushed hard against the anger churning deep in his gut, his composure crumbling with every breath he took. They had worked this case for months, putting the pieces together to finally make an arrest and now they're saying there wasn't enough evidence?

He shook his head. "No. This is not happening. I know he's the one who attacked that woman and he practically confessed to killing those other two women in Hyde Park. I need to talk to the captain." He jerked away from his desk and headed down the hall.

Craig stormed into the office without knocking. "Captain, we cannot let Thomas James walk! We have evidence that ties him to two murders and Joyce Sanders identified him as the guy who attacked her." Craig paced in front of the captain's desk and stopped. "She told us he's been showing up at her house, despite the restraining order."

The captain removed his glasses and laid them on top of the file he'd been going through before Craig barged into the office. "She recanted her statement," he said. "We had to let him go."

Heat surged through Craig's body as if he were standing near a roaring fire. He had worked his ass off on this case, not eating, losing sleep, and even put his badge on the line at times all in the name of solving the case.

A bitter, bark of laughter gushed from the pit of his stomach and he glanced around, waiting for someone to jump out and say "gotcha." There was no way this case could be falling apart with the evidence they had collected over the last few weeks. Thomas James was their guy and Craig would bet his life on that.

The captain stood, walked around the desk and sat on the edge of it, his arms folded across his chest. "I was getting ready to call you in here." He studied Craig for a long moment before saying, "You're off the case, Logan. You're too close to this one and taking the case way too personal."

"What?" Craig yelled. "Captain, how else am I supposed to act when this asshole has killed two defenseless women and is terrorizing another?"

"There's not enough evidence to link him to those two murders. All circumstantial."

Craig threw up his arms. "How can you pull me off when—"

"You're off the case!" the captain barked. "Now go home!"

Craig clenched and unclenched his fists as he glared at the man who had mentored him throughout his career. He knew the captain was doing what he thought was best, but a rebellious rage surged through Craig's veins at the thought of them letting a killer go free. He turned without saying another word and stalked out of the office.

"I'll catch you later," Craig said to Floyd and snatched his jacket from the back of the chair not giving his partner an opportunity to ask him any questions.

Craig slowed when he saw Thomas James leaving with his lawyer.

"Attorney Andrews, may I speak to your client for a minute?" Craig asked.

The lawyer looked from him to Thomas and then back at him after Thomas nodded a confirmation. Andrews stepped off to the side and pulled out his cell phone.

"Officer Logan, so what you gon' do now? Try to accuse me of yet another murder?" Thomas mocked.

Craig hesitated, feeling the urge to punch him in the face, but he knew the act would get him suspended at best and definitely a lawsuit.

"Craig, don't do this," Floyd said close to his ear. "He's not worth it, man."

He hadn't heard his partner approach, but assured him that everything was under control and he just wanted to talk with Thomas alone. Once Floyd walked away, Craig returned his attention to Thomas.

"I actually came to congratulate you and to tell you to enjoy your freedom. We're letting you walk this time." Craig studied him for a moment, irritated by the cocky smirk on his face. "I don't know when and I don't know how, but I will prove that you're a cold-blooded killer who gets his kicks off torturing women." He started to step away, but stopped. "Oh and I'm sure I'll see you back here soon."

Craig turned and walked away before he did something stupid while Thomas laughed as if he'd just finished watching a Kevin Hart comedy show. As long as he lived, Craig would never understand how someone could kill another human being and not feel a thing.

He climbed into his Land Rover unsure of where he was going, but forty-five minutes later, he was pulling up to Toni's townhouse. Days like this he wanted to quit his job, buy a 100-foot yacht and get lost at sea.

Craig stepped out of his truck and leaned against the driver's side door. He gazed up at the sky. Dark, gloomy clouds loomed above and threatened to bring a storm, but Craig didn't care. He was dealing with his own storm churning in his gut. He drew in a deep breath of the cool evening air and thought about Cynthia, his fiancée who was raped and killed by a gang member over four years ago. For years, he'd dedicated his life to ridding the city of men like Thomas James. Men who thought it was okay to hurt and terrorize women. Men who thought they were more of a man by beating on a woman and men who thought they could get away with it. An image of Toni flitted across his mind and his gaze fell on her front door. He would never forget the night she told him how she'd been raped walking home from a party while in college. Young, naive and defenseless, she endured what too many women suffer through on a daily basis and the violence had to stop.

Craig rubbed his forehead and tried to shake loose the feeling of defeat. He couldn't quit the force, but he didn't know what else to do. *You're too close to this one.* The captain's words hit him full force. He was right. Craig had seen the victim, Joyce, and immediately visualized Cynthia and Toni. He had done everything that was humanly possible to put that animal away in order to keep him from hurting another woman … and they let him walk.

"Craig?"

Craig looked up to see Toni climbing out of her work van, the words Jenkins & Sons Construction painted boldly on the side panels. Still standing in the street next to his truck, his gaze raked over her as she approached. Skin the color of toasted caramel glistened with a light sheen while her compelling dark brown eyes studied him as he observed her. He didn't miss the gentle sway of her hips encased in jeans that hugged her generous curves. As far as he was concerned, she was too damn fine to be a plumber. The black and white flannel button-down shirt that hung open revealing a dark T-shirt did nothing to hide the sexy ass body that he knew lie beneath.

"What are you doing here? It's not Friday yet," she joked but sobered when she came closer to him. He wasn't sure what she saw on his face, but he didn't miss the sudden concern in her eyes. "What is it? What's happened? Are you hurt?" Her hands were on his arms and then his chest as she looked him over.

If Craig had any doubt of how she felt about him, those doubts were immediately dispelled by the way she fretted over him now.

He grabbed the hand that rested on his chest and placed a kiss in her palm. "I'm okay," he said allowing the words to roll off his tongue despite the pain in his heart.

She studied him a second longer. "You don't look okay."

The events of the past hour came rushing back and an intense desolation swept through his body. He wasn't sure why he'd driven to her house, but for whatever reason, he had a sudden urge to leave, not wanting her to see him like this. He pushed away from the door and turned, prepared to climb into his truck and go back the way he came. "I shouldn't have come."

She quickly stepped between him and his truck. "You're here now." She reached for his arm and tugged gently. "Come on. Come inside."

CHAPTER FIVE

Toni was surprised to arrive home and find Craig standing in the street, leaning against his truck. At first glance, she thought something across the street had caught his attention, but upon closer inspection, she noticed the vacant look in his eyes. She hadn't seen that haunted expression since the day of Julien's funeral and she feared something was terribly wrong.

"Can I get you something to drink?" She watched him as he strolled around her living room. When she moved out of his house, she moved in with Peyton for a few weeks then purchased the three-level townhouse. Craig hadn't seen her place since the day he brought over a box that she'd left at his house, and even then he'd left the box downstairs near the front door. "Are you hungry?"

He shook his head. "No. I'm good, but thanks."

He stood across the room, staring aimlessly at the wall-to-wall fish tank. The soothing gurgle of the tank's filter and the soft light bouncing off the sky-blue background always brought comfort to Toni whenever she was troubled. She hoped it had the same effect on Craig.

He watched as the fish, big and small swam back and forth around the plastic plants, under the ornamental bridge and around the other props, stopping periodically to stare back at him. He hadn't said much since walking in, but it was as if she could feel his pain seeping through his pores.

"Do you want to talk about what's bothering you?" She asked once he took a seat on the sofa. She sat on the arm of the sofa facing him.

Craig leaned forward, his fingers steepled beneath his chin. He released a noisy sigh and for a while she thought he wasn't going to share what was troubling him, but then he spoke. "I got pulled off a case today."

She waited for him to continue, but when he didn't she said, "And?"

"And it's a first. Captain said I was too close to this case, taking it too personal. It started because of a domestic violence call, but we had evidence that could link the boyfriend to two murder cases." He shook his head and rubbed his eyes. "Captain let him walk this afternoon claiming we didn't have enough to justify holding him and I blew a gasket. I couldn't believe they let him walk."

Toni didn't know what to say. Craig took his job very seriously and anyone who knew him well knew that he had no tolerance for crimes against women. She still remembered his reaction when she told him about her rape. He was just as emotional as she was and she had no doubt that if he could have hunted the bastard down who had taken her innocence he would make him pay.

Craig sat back against the sofa, his large hand rubbing her thigh, sending jolts of pleasure through her body.

"When I was leaving the station all I could think about was you and Cynthia. What you two went through." He looked up at her and the anguish she saw in his eyes made her heart constrict. "I know in my gut that this guy will strike again, and there isn't a damn thing I can do about it."

"Oh, Craig, honey," she covered his hand with hers and squeezed, "you're only one man. You can't protect us all."

He removed his hand from her grasp and pinched the bridge of his nose, laying his head against the back of the sofa. He closed his eyes and Toni felt helpless seeing the pain etched on his face. She didn't know how to help him since she was dealing with her own issues.

For the past hour, she'd been reeling after an argument with her father about bringing Ronald to her grandfather's party. Her and her father's relationship was already shaky, so it didn't take much for her to disappoint him despite being his only child. Her mother had two daughters from a previous marriage and Toni always felt like Cinderella. But instead of a wicked stepmother, Toni had a pain-in-the-butt father who was good at pointing out her flaws and a mother who went along with whatever Toni's father said.

Toni glanced at Craig who appeared to be asleep, but she knew better. He was shutting down. She'd witness the technique many times when he'd come home late from a frustrated day of work. If she didn't get Craig to open up, he would shut her out completely.

"What can I do to make you feel better?" She knew it was a loaded question, but she couldn't stand to see him hurting.

He slowly opened his beautiful hazel eyes and met her gaze. A sensuous light passed between them and Toni knew at that moment that he could ask her for anything and she would do it.

Without a word, he slid his arm beneath her butt and pulled her onto his lap. She gulped hard, afraid of the lustful desires flowing through her body.

Not taking his eyes from hers, Craig ran his hand over her hair and released the clip that held her ponytail in place. His fingers sifted through the long strands.

"God, I love you." He tilted her back into his arms and covered her mouth with his. All her thoughts jumbled together. His kiss, so tender she almost cried. Terrible regrets assailed her at the way she had walked away from him months ago. She would never stop loving him. What she felt for him hadn't diminished, but she knew that right now all she could offer Craig was her body.

Without breaking contact, he removed her flannel shirt, laid her back across his lap and slipped his hands underneath her T-shirt. The soothing sounds of the fish tank did nothing to calm her rapid heart rate as she anticipated his next move. Her breasts surged at the intimacy of his sudden touch against her lace bra, and she squirmed beneath his masterful hand. Heat plowed through her body and a moan sounded from the back of her throat when his fingers circled and tweaked her sensitive nipples. She hadn't been with a man since the last time she'd been with Craig and right now she needed him worse than the desert needed rain.

His kiss was thorough, unhurried, and Toni nearly jumped out of her skin when he unsnapped the front of her bra and her breasts spilled into his large hands. He cupped them with just the right amount of intensity.

"Craig," she panted, not sure what she wanted to say, her mind suddenly blank. He removed her T-shirt in one smooth yank and his mouth went back to work. She had missed their long conversations over coffee and their sometimes heated disagreements, but what she missed most was the way he made her body come alive. He rested his hand on her torso, his thumb making circular motions against her blazing skin while his lips planted a delicious trail of kisses down her neck and then to her collarbone.

"Mmm, you smell good," he growled, nipping at her skin. He scooted to the side and laid her flat on the sofa, his eyes caressed her body. "You have no idea how much I've missed you." He straddled her and shook out of his jacket. He placed his gun and holster on the coffee table then stripped out of his shirt and T-shirt. Her eyes zoned in on his broad shoulders and muscular chest, unable to stop her hands from reaching out and pulling him down on top of her.

"I've missed you too." She lifted her hips, grinding them sensually against his body. She ignored the small voice in her head that demanded she slow her roll. If this were anyone other than Craig on top of her, she might've been able to, but this was Craig and she didn't want to stop. She wanted him even more than she cared to admit.

The doorbell rang.

"Don't answer it," his words gruff against her lips. His hands were like a heat-seeking missile as he undid her belt, and unzipped her jeans with the ease of a person who knew of the gift that lied beneath. "They'll go away."

The bell rang again followed by an insistent knock and Toni wanted to scream. She tried to ignore the pounding but groaned and eventually went limp in Craig's arms. "I'm sorry, but if I don't go see what's going on this person may never go away." When he loosened his hold, she jumped up and slipped on her flannel shirt, only buttoning two of the buttons and zipped her pants. "I'll only be a minute."

She headed toward the stairs that led to the ground floor and glanced back at Craig sitting on her sofa. Her breath caught and her panties grew wetter when he met her gaze as he cupped the large bulge in his pants.

This better be important. She flew down the stairs ready to strangle whoever was leaning on her doorbell and banging on her door.

Once downstairs, she peeked out the window. *What the heck?*

"Ronald, what are you doing here?" she spat out the words impatiently when she swung the door open. She glanced back to make sure Craig hadn't followed her. "I told you I didn't want to see you anymore." If only she had thought to bring her bat downstairs. Apparently, a knock upside the head was the only thing he would understand.

"Come on, baby, you've been dodging me for the past few days. I told you I was sorry about last weekend." He ran a finger down the front of her shirt, between her breast, and she jumped back and held her shirt closed remembering she was braless. "I told you the truth. I forgot I took some allergy medicine earlier that day, and I guess it didn't mix well with liquor."

"What part of I don't want to see you anymore don't you understand?"

"I know what you said, but I know you didn't mean it. You have to give me another chance."

"Ronald, we're done. Now leave before I call the police."

"Oh, so now you're threatening me?" He stepped closer and backed her into the entryway. A wicked sneer marred his handsome face as he loomed over her. "I said I was sorry. What more do you want?"

"I want you to leave. Now!"

She knew all she had to do was call out to Craig, but knowing how protective he was of her and the mood he was in when he arrived, she figured she'd try to handle Ronald herself.

"I know you're into me." He leaned down to kiss her, but she turned her head. His features hardened and he grabbed her chin in his hand, pulling her closer. "I don't think I want to leave."

"Then you might want to rethink that." Craig's deep baritone voice was low and deadly. Toni knew that all Craig needed today was an excuse to punch someone.

Ronald jerked his head up. "Who the hell are you?" he growled. "This is between me and her, so you can just go back to wherever you came from. Or better yet, why don't you show yourself out and stay out of our business."

Toni didn't have to look around to know that Craig was standing directly behind her, his anger breathing down her neck.

Craig stepped around her, one of his hands shoved into his front pants pocket. "I can't believe you showed up here, despite Toni telling you over and over again that she's not interested in you." He shook his head. "Damn, man, you're even stupider than I originally thought."

Toni grabbed Craig's arm when he moved closer to Ronald. "Craig, please don't ..." She quickly turned to Ronald knowing what Craig was capable of. "Just leave before you get hurt."

"Oh, please," Ronald snapped. "Like this pretty-boy's going to do anything. I'll leave when I get good and ready." He leaned against the coat-closet door and folded his arms across his chest.

Craig grabbed his arm. "You heard the lady. Get out."

"Man, you don't know me!" Ronald yanked free and pointed his finger in Craig's face. "And you sure as hell don't scare me! So I suggest you leave before *you're* the one who gets hurt."

Ronald eased his jacket open and that's when Toni noticed the dark handle of the weapon sticking out of the front of his waistband.

Craig pulled a gun out of thin air. "Police officer, freeze! Let me see your hands, asshole!" His gun was aimed at Ronald and Ronald seemed to be just as stunned as Toni. "I said let me see your goddamn hands!"

Ronald slowly lifted his hands and backed away until he bumped into the wall near the door. "You're a cop?" he asked in disbelief. Craig snatched Ronald's gun from the front of his pants and shoved it into the back of his waistband, not taking his eyes off him. Ronald turned his attention to Toni. "You set me up?"

Toni shook her head stunned at the way the situation was turning out. "No, no ... I ... I ..."

"Toni, go upstairs and call 911."

"Craig." She was afraid to leave them alone. She knew Craig was the ultimate professional, taking his job seriously and wouldn't do anything to jeopardize his livelihood. But she also knew he was hurting and disappointed in the way his case turned out. She feared he would snap at any moment. Ronald showing up didn't help the situation.

"Go now, Toni!" Rarely did he raise his voice at her, but the vibrations from his anger bounced off the walls and Toni stumbled, but quickly found her footing.

She slowly backed up the stairs and heard Craig say to Ronald, "I ought to put a bullet in your head for harassing her."

***

Anger sent a blast of adrenaline spiraling through Craig's body. He flexed his hands on the steel barrel of his gun, drew in a deep breath and fought hard to fill his constricted lungs. He itched to pull the trigger and that scared him to death. He couldn't make this jerk take the blame for all of the other bastards who threatened women and got away with it. But to find him threatening Toni, made him want to do unthinkable things to him.

"I didn't do anything. Why'd you have her call 911?"

"What do you mean you didn't do anything? You've been harassing her, you came here and threatened her, and you've been following her." Craig cracked a devious smile at the surprised look on Ronald's face. "Yeah, I know what you've been up to the last few days."

"Hey, I meant no harm." He lowered his hands. "I was trying to plead my case. I wasn't going to do anything to Toni." His gaze darted around the small space.

"Yeah, that's why you're carrying a gun. Keep your hands where I can see them." Ronald raised his hands higher. "You might have to do this shit to get women to date you, but when you start harassing *my* woman, you've gone too far."

"Your ... your woman?" His eyebrows shot up. "I didn't know. She didn't say she was seeing anyone."

"It doesn't matter. You should have left her alone when she first told you to. Now I'm going to charge you with everything from carrying a concealed weapon to assault, since I witnessed you threaten her."

Two police officers arrived before Craig could finish his speech.

"What's up, Detective Logan?" The tall lanky officer with a spattering of freckles across the bridge of his nose greeted Craig. "I see you're catching bad guys even when you're off duty huh?"

Craig offered a slight smile and nodded, but didn't take his eyes off Ronald while the cops read him his Miranda rights. After they had him cuffed, Craig leaned close to Ronald.

"Come near her again, and I will beat your ass so bad no one's going to be able to identify your body."

"Wh ... what?" Ronald glanced around frantically. "Did you hear what he said to me?" He yelled at the cop pushing him toward the squad car.

"Hear what?" the officer turned to his partner. "Did you hear anything?"

"Nope. Not a thing. Let's go."

"Did you have to arrest him?" Toni asked when they walked back upstairs, the disapproval in her tone evidence that she didn't like the way he handled the situation.

Craig frowned at her. "That jerk was threatening you and now you're asking me why I did everything I could to make sure you're protected?"

She rocked on the balls of her feet, her hands shoved inside her back pockets. "I guess not. I just wish things could have been handled differently."

Craig slipped into his jacket not taking his gaze off Toni. He wanted more than anything to carry her to her bedroom and pick up where they left off minutes ago, but he was glad Ronald had interrupted their little tryst. He had lost his head. Getting her back in his life was going to take time and finesse. He wasn't the most patient man in the world, but he had to figure out why she really left him and then determine how best to convince her to give him another chance. To give them another chance.

He grabbed her hand and led her back down the stairs and to the door. Leaving was the last thing he wanted to do, but it was too soon for them to have sex. Even a kiss was pushing the limit when he considered each time their lips touched, he wanted to ravage other parts of her body. Nothing had been settled between them and once he won her back, he wanted all of her. Not the woman who was apparently keeping a secret that she thought he couldn't handle.

He pulled her into his arms. "I'm sorry about showing up today the way I did, but I'm not going to apologize for what happened to Ronald. I've seen too many situations go horribly wrong because some knucklehead wanted to scare a woman into submission. You mean everything to me, and there is no way I'm going to let anyone get away with harassing you."

Toni leaned into his touch. "I'm glad you were here." Her hands rested against his chest and he could feel the heat from her fingers through his shirt. "You know you don't have to leave right?" Her hands inched up his chest until she reached his shoulders and wrapped her arms around his neck.

He backed her up against the wall and rubbed his lower body against hers, making sure she felt the effect she had on him. "I would love to stay, but I need to go down to the station and give my report." He nuzzled her neck while his hands explored her curves, his shaft growing harder against his zipper by her erotic moans. He loved the way her body molded into his, but if he didn't stop now, he was going to take her right then and there.

He placed a lingering kiss against her soft lips and pulled back. "Until Friday."

CHAPTER SIX

Toni's fresh scent of *Cashmere Mist* permeated the air, and all Craig could think about was pulling her into his arms and kissing her senseless. She'd worn the same mellow fragrance of airy sandalwood, mixed with baby powder the first time he made love to her. The scent drove him crazy then, and it had the same effect now. He wondered if she wore the perfume intentionally to entice him.

"You didn't get rid of the Camaro did you?" Toni asked when they stopped next to the Land Rover with chrome rims and dark tinted windows. "I didn't get a chance to ask you the other day when you stopped by."

"No, I still have Red Rage. She's the jewel of my collection. I needed a vehicle that handled better in the snow and besides that the Rover is plusher. Do you like it?"

"I do, and it's nice to see you're finally using some of your inheritance to buy a few toys," she said sliding onto the soft leather seat. "Can I drive?" she asked before he shut her door.

Craig laughed. The last time he had let her drive his Camaro, not only did she scare the crap out of him but she was pulled over for speeding. It was a good thing he was in the passenger seat.

"Uh, we'll see," he said when he slid into the driver's side.

Tonight he wanted them to hash out their differences and get to the bottom of what was bothering her, find out what was keeping her from being his again. The sexual attraction between them was stronger than ever, but the conversations over the last few days proved that they were still on different sides when it came to getting back together. As far as he was concerned, they were a perfect couple and he still didn't buy her reason for breaking up with him in the first place, especially when even now he felt that powerful connection that they'd once had.

Twenty minutes later, Craig pulled into the underground parking lot of the Hilton Cincinnati Netherland Plaza. He escorted Toni through the main lobby not missing the way her eyes lit up as she perused the architectural detail of the historic building. She was the only woman he knew who got off on architectural structures. Each time he brought her to the building it was as if she had an orgasmic experience when she walked through. Not only did she admire the Brazilian rosewood, the Egyptian décor, and the Rookwood fountain that made up the exquisite masterpiece, on occasion, she felt it her duty to inform him of the history of the building.

"I don't think I'll ever tire of being in the midst of such perfection," Toni said wistfully.

Craig placed his hand at the small of her back, pulling her closer. "I'm glad you think I'm perfect," he said near her ear. "I think you're pretty perfect yourself."

She swatted at him and laughed. "I was actually talking about the plaza and you know it."

He chuckled. "All I know is that whenever we're together, you look at me with those exotic brown eyes like you want to jump my bones and have your way with me."

She slowed and her mouth dropped opened as if she'd been caught watching her parents have sex.

Well, well, well, I didn't just imagine the looks she gave me the night of her grandfather's party and the other day at her place. Craig placed the new knowledge of how Toni wanted him into the back of his mind and gently nudged her along toward the restaurant before she could reply. Instead of taking her to dinner, maybe what he should have done was get a hotel room.

"Good evening. Thank you for joining us here at Orchids at Palm Court. Do you have a reservation?" the hostess asked.

"Yes. Our reservation should be under Logan."

"Ah, yes, here we are." She scribbled something on the board lying in front of her, grabbed two menus and handed them to the hostess to her right. "Melanie will show you to your table."

"Thank you."

"Is this table okay?" Melanie asked when they reached a semi-circle booth slightly hidden by a palm tree secluded from the other tables.

Craig glanced at Toni for her approval. When she nodded he agreed, "This is perfect, thank you."

Craig and Toni talked and laughed like old times throughout dinner, and Craig realized just how much he had missed their conversations. No other woman stimulated him the way Toni did, mentally or physically. Her quirky sense of humor, her contagious smile and her ability to speak on any subject made him want to be around her all the time. He missed living with her. He missed knowing that when he got off a long, stressful work shift, she was in his home waiting for him, willing to talk and listen as only a significant other could do. This was the woman he wanted to spend the rest of his life with.

"So how's the construction business?" Craig asked.

"What? Peyton didn't tell you?" Toni smirked and moved her plate aside. She folded her hands on top of the table and tilted her head. "From what I can tell, it sounds like you and some of the members of my family have stayed in contact despite our breakup."

Craig chuckled. "What can I say? Your family became my family when we were dating, and though you asked me to give you the space you needed, I didn't see anything wrong with maintaining my friendship with the Jenkins clan."

Slow to speak, Toni brushed a few crumbs off to the side with the back of her hand. Seconds passed before she lifted her eyes to him. "I'm sorry ... for everything. I know when I told you I needed space and then moved out you were caught off guard. I realize now, I should have handled the situation differently."

Craig leaned forward and covered her hands with his. "What would you have done differently?" He thought this might be his only opportunity to find out what triggered her decision.

Toni shook her head. "I'm not sure. Maybe I would have actually sat down and tried to explain how I was feeling. I'm just not sure."

Craig knew if he pushed too hard she would push back. He also knew that they would never be able to move forward if she wasn't honest with her feelings. He released her small hands. He was always amazed at their softness considering she made a living as a plumber.

"You know ..." He stopped speaking when the busboy came to clear their table, followed by the server.

"How was dinner tonight?" She looked at Toni and then at him.

"Good," Craig said.

"Good as usual," Toni added.

"I'm glad to hear that. How about some dessert this evening?"

The server rattled off their dessert menu and the items she'd recommend. All Craig could think about was the type of dessert he wanted. The type that wasn't on the menu. What he wouldn't give to spend the night with Toni and get reacquainted with her luscious body, feel her soft skin against his and come together as one, with him deep inside her sweet heat.

"Craig?" Toni called his name more than once. "The server asked if you wanted anything."

He shook off the vision of Toni lying naked beneath him. "Uh coffee, just coffee."

When the server walked away with their order Craig asked, "What was your real reason for breaking up with me, for walking away from a relationship that was better than good?"

His gaze clung to hers, analyzing her reaction to his question, but then she glanced away.

"So when did you make detective?" Toni asked finally looking at him.

Craig knew how she felt about his job and planned to stay clear of all conversation regarding his work. But why evade the inevitable? The evening was not going according to plan anyway.

"A couple of months ago." He ran a slow hand down his goatee and held her gaze. "I took the test shortly after we broke up and," he shrugged "now I'm a detective."

He watched as she traced the rim of her wine glass with her finger apparently in deep thought. Craig took that opportunity to admire how hot she looked tonight. Like him, Toni favored jeans, T-shirt and anything else that made her comfortable. So the times when she wore makeup and a make-a-brother-weak-in-the-knees dress, like the gold and black number she had on now, it was as if she were transformed into a different person. His gaze zoned in on her more-than-a-handful breasts and recalled how the two works-of-art felt in his hands and tasted against his tongue. The woman was sexy as all get-out and he was having a hard time sitting near her without wanting to be between her thighs.

"What's the difference between a police officer and a police detective?" Toni asked, pulling him back into the conversation. "Is being a detective less dangerous?"

Craig diverted his eyes to his hand as he tapped his finger on the table, the sound muffled by the thick white tablecloth. What could he tell her? Both positions were demanding, stressful and at times dangerous. He knew she didn't want to hear that and he couldn't think of a way to sugarcoat a detective's risks.

"Be honest with me," she added.

Craig met her gaze and wasn't sure what he saw. Hope? Concern? Maybe fear. He never lied to her and he didn't plan to start now.

"Police officers have a higher instance of on-the-job injuries since their main responsibility is to protect people and property. My main responsibility as a detective is to gather facts and evidence of crimes. I might not necessarily face danger the way a police officer might, but there are times when detectives walk into dangerous situations unknowingly."

"I see."

"Do you?" He leaned forward and placed his forearms on the table. "Or are you still trying to find an excuse to keep us apart? Because if you are, let me tell you something. I've missed you. That's what this," he waived a hand drawing her attention to their surroundings, "is all about. I want you to remember how good we were together and ... I want what we once had and I think you do to."

She lifted her water glass to her lips, peering over the rim at him.

"Craig, we've already been through this," she said and sat her glass back down. "We agreed that this, just being friends, was for the best."

He shook his head and leaned back in his seat. "No, *we* didn't agree. The breakup was all you. One night out of nowhere, you told me you couldn't date a cop. Mind you, your declaration was after we'd lived together for over six months. I've been on the force for over seven years and you knew my occupation and the element of danger when you entered our relationship."

Toni pulled her bottom lip between her teeth, which was something she did often when she was nervous. Her eyes studied her hands, interlocked on top of the table.

"Yes I knew, but the reality didn't hit me of just how dangerous your job was until you ended up in the hospital from a gunshot wound." She lifted her eyes to his. "When I found out Julien was killed ... and you two had been together ... Craig, I couldn't handle the risk," she said in a voice laced with anguish, her eyes filled with unshed tears.

She was still in love with him. She had to be. Otherwise, she wouldn't be on the verge of tears. He still wasn't buying that the risk was her only reason for walking away from what they once shared, but he had no doubt that the danger played a role in her decision.

He watched as she sucked in a deep breath and used her cloth napkin to dab at her eyes. The last thing he wanted was for her to relive the night that he was shot. Hell, the last thing he wanted was to relive that night. Had he known better, there were so many things he would have done differently. His biggest mistake — he shouldn't have had his brother call her to the hospital. Craig had no idea she'd freak out the way she had. In the year that they had dated, six months of that time living under the same roof, he had never seen her fall apart the way she had when he was shot. And even more so when she found out his partner had been killed. That was the worst night of Craig's life. Not only did he lose his friend and partner of five years, but that night was also the beginning of Toni slowly pulling away from him.

***

Toni took a fortifying breath and glanced around her favorite restaurant, trying to pull herself together. Craig was giving her the perfect opportunity to tell him her real reason for walking away from him that night, giving her an opportunity to tell him what else happened that horrible night she was raped. If only she had the courage.

"Toni."

She toyed with the napkin in her lap before speaking. "You don't know what it's like to watch you leave for work and not know if I'm going to see you later. Wondering whether or not someone is going to knock on the door and tell me that you've been killed. You don't know what that feels like."

A few tears slipped down her cheeks and the faster she wiped them away, the faster they fell. She had a love-hate relationship with him being a cop. On one hand, she was glad the police force had men like him who truly gave their all to protect innocent people, but on the other hand, she feared for his life daily.

Craig moved to sit next to her, pulling her into his arms. He alerted the server and asked for the check while he gently rocked Toni in his arms.

"I'm so sorry, baby." He lifted her chin. "I hate the thought of you living in fear because of my career, but you have to understand, I went through the same thing whenever you walked out the door." He wiped her tears with the pad of his thumb. "I know the evil that lurks on our city streets. I see things on a daily basis that would make you want to get out of town quick or maybe even leave the country. When I show up at a crime scene of a woman who decided to give her abusive husband another chance, then she ends up dead or a woman who has been brutally raped and then left for dead, I know that she could have easily been you. So baby, you're not the only one who lives in fear."

He paid for dinner and then slid out of the booth, his hand outstretched to her. "Let's get out of here."

Toni road the entire way home thinking about Craig's words, *you're not the only one who lives in fear*. Of all the stories he'd told her while they were dating, never had he mentioned he feared for her life. Sure he complained about her going on service calls by herself, not knowing what type of customer she might encounter, but she didn't know how deep his fear for her safety ran.

"Are you okay?" Craig asked when he pulled up to her townhouse.

She assured him that she was fine and waited until he walked around to the passenger side of the truck and practically lifted her out. They strolled up the walkway toward the entrance of her townhouse, Craig following closely behind her. The tension in her body slowly began to ease when he agreed not to rush her into making a decision about them.

She glanced up at the red brick three-level structure, accentuated with an arched doorway and domed windows and fell in love with the place again each time she arrived home.

"Thanks for tonight, Craig," she said as they approached the front stoop. "Sorry about all the tears. I hope I didn't make your evening too uncomfortable."

He pulled her into his arms, not giving her a chance to protest. "Though I hate when you cry, I hope you know that I'll always have a shoulder for you to cry on."

She met his gaze and knew she would never really be over him. If his words and actions weren't enough to make her believe his feelings for her, the love she saw brimming in his gorgeous eyes let her know that she still held a special spot in his heart.

"Thank you."

Craig caressed her cheek and the gentleness of his touch sent goose bumps up and down her arms. She should pull away from him knowing how quickly her body responded to his touch, but she couldn't.

"Do you want to come in?" she asked in a hoarse whisper, her body pulsing by his nearness.

He studied her for what seemed like an hour, but was mere seconds before speaking. "That probably wouldn't be a good idea. I want you back in my life Toni. All of you. I know if I walk across that threshold, I won't be able to stop myself from devouring you."

She lifted her hands to his chest, his taut muscles jumped beneath her touch and she knew she wanted him as bad as he claimed to want her. More importantly, she wanted him back in her life too.

"I think I want you to devour me," she said without meeting his gaze. "I've missed you so—

Craig lowered his head and his mouth swooped down over hers. Toni knew no more words were needed. What had she been thinking walking away from this remarkable man? The other day, after he had taken care of Ronald, she had promised herself that she wouldn't just fall back into his arms, but in the last few days, images of him had invaded her dreams, reminding her of happier times, amazing conversations and unbelievable sex.

"Maybe we should take this inside," she said when she reluctantly pulled away. "I don't want my neighbors to call the police on you."

Craig chuckled. "Let 'em call. I know people."

Toni unlocked the door trying to keep the voice of reason at bay. After one date, that really wasn't a date but her fulfilling payment for blackmail, she was ready to share her bed with him again. She wanted to believe her desire was ignited because she hadn't had sex since they broke up, but she knew the longing was more than that. She missed him. She needed him. She was still in love with him.

When they made their way up the stairs, Toni placed her handbag and keys on the bookshelf and then turned to Craig who was standing so closely behind her that she bumped into him. Without a word, he gripped the back of her thighs and hoisted her up into his arms. She wrapped her legs around his waist not caring that her short dress was hiked up and that her lace panties were probably showing. All she knew was that she wanted to be as close to him as possible.

She curved one arm around his neck, her hand stroking the back of his head as she placed a lingering kiss on his forehead, against his smooth jaw and then on his inviting lips. Her stomach clenched and a sweet heat pulsed through her veins when he said, "I love you" against her lips.

"I love you too," her finger outlined his perfectly shaped mustache and worked its way down to his sexy goatee. She zoned in on his tempting mouth and ran her thumb across his bottom lip before she captured it gently between her teeth.

He tightened his hold on her and groaned when she slipped her tongue between his lips, coaxing, caressing, and making love to his mouth in a way that left no doubt to what she wanted. Their kiss started out gentle but quickly heated up and spun out of control.

"Baby, I pride myself on having control when it comes to getting inside of you," Craig said between ragged breaths, "but if you keep this up, I'm going to take you right here and right now against this wall. When what I really want is to take my time, get reacquainted with your beautiful body and make sweet passionate love to you."

"Oookay," she said softly, her senses spinning out of control as he squeezed and massaged her butt cheeks, the intensity in his eyes holding her captive. "You … uh … you might want to put me down first since my bedroom is on the third floor and there are tons of stairs."

"Despite a certain amount of discomfort from a part of my anatomy that is straining against my zipper, thanks to you, I think I can manage. Just point me in the right direction."

Craig carried her effortlessly up the stairs, down the hall and didn't stop until he reached her bedroom. He set her on her feet near the bed and picked up where he'd left off downstairs.

"Are you sure about this?" he mumbled against her skin, his lips searing a fiery path down her neck, his hands held her close, one on her bare back, the other gripped her ass. "Because baby if you're not sure, you better stop me now."

Toni was barely able to breathe, let alone speak. His mouth and hands scorched her heated flesh.

"I'm … I'm sure," she moaned. She knew there was no turning back and if she let Craig back into her bed, she was letting him back into her life. Living without him for the past few months had been unbearably lonely. Now he was back doing wicked things with his tongue and hands. Oh, yeah, she was definitely sure. She wanted this. She wanted him.

CHAPTER SEVEN

Craig slid the thin straps of her dress from her shoulders, his gaze holding hers as his fingers grazed her torrid skin. Prickles of desire raced down her arms and a shiver gripped her body when his pink tongue slipped out and swiped at his lower lip. She swallowed hard knowing what all his tongue was capable of, and what she was sure to experience tonight. After walking away from him months ago, she honestly didn't think she would be where she was now. Staring at the only man who had ever made her feel like a precious gift, anticipating a night of passion that she had fantasized about for months.

Her dress puddled to the floor and Craig took a step back, his hungry gaze traveled from her bare breasts down to the skimpy lace that covered her most prized possession. The fire in his hazel eyes ignited sensations within Toni that made her panties wet and her sex throb. If he didn't make a move soon, she was taking matters into her own hands.

"I think you're even more beautiful than I remember." The sensual tone in his voice matched the admiring gaze that raked over her boldly.

"And I think you have on way too many clothes." She moved forward as he shook out of his suit jacket, tossing it in a nearby chair and then started on the buttons of his shirt. "Here, let me."

She moved her hands from his narrow waist up to his muscular chest, her nimble fingers unbuttoning the last few buttons on his dress shirt. She peeled the shirt slowly off his broad shoulders and let it drop to the floor. Things were going fine until Craig placed his hands on her hips and his lips against the curve of her neck. He knew the areas on her body that brought her the most pleasure and the sweet torture of his mouth, his tongue stroking and his lips nipping the skin between her neck and shoulder blade, was almost her undoing.

"Craig," she moaned when he pulled her closer and ground his hard body against hers in a slow seductive rhythm that nearly brought her to her knees. The desire raging through her body outweighed the friction of his pants against her skimpy panties as her hands explored the hollows of his back and worked their way down to his firm butt, feeling his erection against her stomach. "Craig," she muttered, her trembling limbs clung to him.

"I'm right here, baby." He lifted her with one swift move and placed her on the bed. "And I'm not leaving until I hear you scream my name over and over again."

He removed a condom from his wallet and placed the foiled packet on the nightstand, and then made quick work of dropping his pants and his briefs. The mattress dipped under his weight and before Toni could respond to his last comment, his mouth closed around her taut nipple, shutting down any coherent thoughts. A burning need swept through her, setting her body on fire.

"Craig," she whined when his hands seared a path down her abdomen and onto her thigh, his touch light and painfully teasing. She appreciated the whole seduction thing, but she wanted him closer. Now!

"I know what you want," he said as if reading her mind, "but I told you earlier, I plan to take my time with you tonight, get reacquainted with your body and make love to you like I used to, slowly and completely."

"No, no, Craig," she panted, wiggling beneath him as his mouth trailed kisses over her stomach, then lower and then even lower. "I need you inside me." She grabbed hold of his arms, forcing him back up her body until they were face to face and his body covered hers. She gripped his face, panting and looked him in the eyes. "I ... want ... you .... now."

A sexy grin tilted the corner of his mouth and he chuckled. "I love when you tell me what you want."

He moved to her side and slowly slid her damp panties down her legs and tossed them aside. It was clear that despite her request, he was going to take his own sweet time, not caring that the thought of them coming together had her trembling with anticipation.

Her breath caught when he placed the cold tip of his finger between her breasts and slowly glided it down the center of her body, not stopping until he reached the wisp of hair covering her entrance. *God help me.* The intensity in his eyes as his gaze traveled the length of her body evoked all sorts of sensations. No man had ever made her feel so desired.

Craig turned slightly and retrieved the condom as Toni hungrily devoured his every move. Sheer perfection were the only two words she could think of to describe his amazing body. He was truly the total package and she wondered how she managed to walk away from him months ago.

A hot ache grew between her thighs when Craig's tongue snaked out of his mouth and seductively swiped against his lower lip as he sheathed himself, his eyes glued to hers.

"Are you sure you're ready for me?"

She wanted to scream *hell yeah* but all she could manage was a jerky nod as he climbed on top of her. He cupped her breasts between his large hands and pushed them together, his tongue circling wickedly over her nipples. Her eyes shuddered closed as his mouth continued to make tender love to her breasts, sending a sweet sensation through her body and turning her insides to mush. At this rate, she didn't know how much she could handle tonight.

When his finger grazed her sensitive opening, she practically leaped off the bed, but he held her firm. "Oh, yeah, you're ready," he whispered hoarsely, inserting one finger into her smoldering heat and then two.

"Ohh," Toni whimpered, her head thrashing against the pillow, barely hanging on as his fingers pumped deeper and deeper, swirling and stroking, while his thumb teased her delicate pearl. Toni squeezed her eyes closed, her pulse pounded in her ear as she struggled to hold on, but felt herself slipping off the edge of reality. She bucked against his hand and her resistance encouraged him to continue the sweet torture to her body.

"That's it baby, just let go," Craig coaxed his lips tracing a path over her skin. He amped up the pressure, and uncontrolled passion shot through her and the hysteria of delight pushed her over the edge.

"Craig!" she screamed, her nails clawing at his shoulders as wave after wave of pleasure roared through her body, shattering any control she thought she had. She shook viciously against his hand, gasping for air as he repositioned his body over hers.

Before she could catch her breath, he nudged her thighs wider and buried his thick length inside of her without warning. "Craig!" she cried, her rapid breaths sounded loud to her own ears as he filled her completely, her body adjusting to his size.

"Damn baby, you're tight. Am I hurting you?" He slowed his moves.

"No. No," she said through shallow breaths gripping his butt and forcing him to keep moving. "Please, please don't stop."

The dulcet ache of ecstasy throbbed through her as he rotated his hips and increased his pace, whispering hoarsely all the things he planned to do to her body. How many nights had she laid awake longing for the delicious torture of him plunging deeper and deeper inside her?

She gripped a handful of the sheets as waves of pleasure grew like a brewing storm over the Atlantic Ocean as Craig continued to slide in and out of her, taking her to new heights with every stroke. His thrust became harder and faster.

"Toni," he said in a warning tone, his pace frantically increasing as she felt him teeter on the edge of his own control. He growled and moved like a man possessed, pounding her into the mattress, his strokes long and powerful.

"Oh my God, Craig!" she screamed at the top of her lungs when a soul-drenching orgasm grabbed hold of her and wouldn't let go, wracking every inch of her body as her world spun out of control. "Ohmygod, ohmygod, ohmygod." Tears clouded her eyes as she struggled to breathe with Craig pumping his hips faster, gripping her butt tighter as his own control began to slip.

"Oh, shiiiiitttt!" He roared, and his body convulsed like a city hit with a magnitude seven earthquake. "Oh shi …" Craig mumbled in the crook of Toni's neck, aftershocks shook his body.

Toni threw her arms around his neck and held onto him tight, her heart still beating at an immeasurable rate.

Minutes passed without either of them speaking until Craig said, "You're mine," he muttered breathlessly against her neck and then rolled onto his back, taking her with him. "You will always be mine."

***

Toni awakened to raindrops slapping against the windowpane and the howling wind blowing hard enough to make a tree branch scratch the side of the building. She had no idea how long she'd been asleep, but outside was still dark and the hard chest beneath her head and the legs tangled with hers, brought the activities of the night back to her. She sighed contently thinking about what the reunion meant.

Unfortunately, experiencing two rounds of amazing sex didn't solve the problem of why she had walked away from their relationship in the first place. There was no way she could make any type of commitment to Craig without telling him everything. Knowing how much he wanted a family made the decision to tell him about the night she was raped that much harder. He already knew she'd been raped, but how could she tell him that after that bastard raped her and then left her bloodied and ashamed, he also left her with another package. A package that nearly broke her. A package that tortured her peace of mind and stripped her innocence away. A package that forced her to make a decision that had forever changed her life.

Toni swallowed hard and forced herself not to cry. Ten years, she'd kept this secret. Her heavy heart felt as if it were breaking all over again. She loved Craig enough to tell him everything, but did he love her enough to understand her decision? Could she risk telling him about the baby?

***

Craig jerked awake first noticing the weight on his arms and then glanced down only to stare into the most beautiful brown eyes he'd ever seen. A gleam of sunlight shimmered off her silky long hair and their extracurricular activities of the night before flooded his mind.

Craig pinched her butt.

"Ouch!" She punched him in the arm. "What'd you do that for?"

Craig threw his head back and laughed. "Last night was amazing. I wanted to make sure all that passion wasn't a dream."

"You know dog-on-well it wasn't a dream." She pouted and pulled away until he stopped her.

"Wait, don't go." Holding her close against his body, he placed a kiss on her nose, then her lips. "I'm sorry. Let me rub it and make it feel better," he teased and gripped her rear-end, rubbing her cheeks gently. "You know, I think this is how we got started last night."

"I think you're right." She squirmed against him as he trailed kisses down her delectable neck, his hand lifting her leg over his thigh.

"We need to talk."

Every man alive dreaded those four words, and he was no different. Last night had been incredible, and he wasn't about to let her ruin their morning by over thinking.

"I don't want to talk." He continued his journey down her neck until he reached her breast, immediately lowering his mouth to one taut nipple. "I'd rather pick up where we left off last night and maybe communicate using our bodies instead of our words," he mumbled against her warm skin.

She moaned and moved with him until she thought about what they were doing. "Craig, I'm serious." She placed her hands on each side of his face and pulled him up, their gazes clashing. "We really do need to talk."

He released a frustrated sigh and threw his head back against the pillows, letting his arms drop to his side. "Toni ... baby, I don't want us talking to ruin what we shared last night. Don't worry, I'm not going to ask you to marry me," he rose slightly and looked at her, "yet, but I am going to ask you to give us another chance."

She cupped her hand against his cheek and kissed his lips. "That's what I want, but I think we should talk first."

Craig sat up and leaned against the headboard, pulling Toni into his arms he kissed the top of her head. "Nah, this is what we're going to do. I'm going to talk and you're going to listen."

"But Craig there's something—"

"There's something special between us and I want us to take things slow, hang out and get to know each other again. One day at a time."

"But ..."

"But right now, I plan to make love to my beautiful woman."

He laid her down on the bed and covered her mouth with his, ceasing all conversation of any doubts she might have had about their reunion. He didn't know what she was afraid of, but for now, he planned to do whatever he could to show her how much he loved her and then he would prove once and for all that they were made for each other.

CHAPTER EIGHT

A wave of giddiness gripped Toni the moment she pulled up to Craig's house. She wasn't sure what had come over her. She grinned like she'd just learned the secret to keeping a manicure fresh for a month. It wasn't like she hadn't seen Craig every day for the past week and a half. Maybe the joy flowing through her veins had something to do with the fact that they were meeting for their first afternoon rendezvous at his place.

She climbed out of her work van and practically floated to the door, and then rang the doorbell.

"Who is it?" Craig asked through the closed door.

"It's the plumber. I've come to fix the sink."

She heard him laugh before he pulled open the door. "You're crazy. Get in here." He tugged her inside and into his arms. Toni couldn't think of any other place she'd rather be than right there molded against his lean body. "Well hello," he mumbled, his lips brushed against hers as he spoke. "I have to admit, you're the finest plumber I've ever laid eyes on. But," he broke off the kiss suddenly and released her, "you have to hurry and take care of that sink problem before my woman gets here. She's the jealous type and doesn't like fine-ass plumbers hanging out in my house."

"Ha, ha, ha, very funny. I see you've got jokes." Toni took off her work boots and followed him into the kitchen.

"So do you use that 'I'm here to fix the sink', line often?" He glanced over his shoulder as he removed a long pan from the oven. "Maybe to pick up unsuspecting men like me?"

"Actually my dear, you're the only man I've used that line on." She wiggled her eyebrows at him and grinned.

He flashed a goofy I'm-the-luckiest-man-in-the-world smile that lit up his hazel eyes and jump-started the giddiness that swirled around inside her body. When he turned back to his delicious smelling dish and sprinkled additional cheese across the top, Toni couldn't help but recall the first plumbing job she did for him, he was cooking then too. A small smile tilted her lips as she admired how easily he moved around the kitchen. Unlike the first time they met, today he didn't have his police uniform on and didn't look as intimidating. She loved a man in uniform, but Craig's tall figure in blue jeans hanging low on his hips and a white tank top showing off thick muscular arms and washboard abs were just as sizzling.

"Ahem."

Toni's gaze shot up to find Craig checking her out and wearing a crooked grin. She swallowed hard and rubbed her sweaty palms down the thighs of her jeans. Hopefully he couldn't read minds. If he could, he would know that she was now imagining him naked.

"Uhh … so what's for lunch?"

Craig sauntered across the room. He pulled her close and nuzzled the side of her neck, his hands easily sliding underneath her T-shirt. "My version of baked Ziti, but now I'm thinking that maybe I should have you for lunch, and we save the Ziti for dessert," he mumbled against her burning skin. "We have about fifteen minutes before I have to take it out of the oven. Just enough time for a quickie."

He backed her up to the granite countertop and her entire body went liquid with anticipation when he lifted her shirt over her head and cupped her breasts, sending a spark of desire straight to her midsection. His mouth covered hers in a deep penetrating kiss as he skimmed his skillful fingers over her lace bra, tweaking her nipples, immediately making them rise to attention. All thoughts of food flew out of Toni's mind and was replaced with a yearning desire to have their bodies joined as one when he paid her other breast the same attention as the first.

Craig lifted his head. "I have to get you out of these clothes," he said, his gruff voice turning her on almost as much as the quick work he did in stripping her out of her jeans, leaving her with only her bra and bikini panties on. He stood back, his hungry gaze raked over her body and lingered on her breasts. "Damn, girl, you're sexy with or without clothes, but right now I need you up higher. Sometimes I forget how short you are without your heels on."

"Craig!" she yelped when, without warning, he lifted her and placed her on the cool granite countertop. "My grandmother would have a fit if she saw me sitting on a kitchen counter. Especially if she knew what we were about to do."

"Well, it's a good thing she's not here." He quirked his eyebrows up and down.

***

Craig tossed his flimsy tank top aside. He'd waited all morning to have Toni in his arms again, imagining all that he would do to her when she arrived. Now that she was there, sitting in her skimpy underwear looking good enough to eat, he planned to have his way with her.

His arms encircled her small waist and he moved his mouth over hers, devouring its softness as his hands slid up and down her feminine curves. Unbelievable need bloomed inside him, but withered when his hand stumbled against the back of her lace bra.

"You look incredible in your underwear, but this has to go," he said of her pink lace bra, the tremble in his voice a sure sign of the erotic effect she was having on him. He chucked the bra over his shoulder, yanked off the little strip of material she called panties and pulled her close. "Now where was I?" Not waiting for a response, he trailed feathery kisses down the length of her scented neck while his fingers teased and tugged one of her swollen nipples. Her whimpers sent his body into overdrive, and the frantic movements of her hands gripping his shoulders fueled the flames that had ignited the moment he stripped off her last stitch of clothing.

"Okay, okay, wait," Toni panted and pushed against his chest, her breasts jiggled as she tried to catch her breath. "It's your turn," she said and waved toward his jeans. "I want them off."

Craig shrugged nonchalantly despite his own breaths coming in short spurts. "If you insist." He backed away and removed a condom from his wallet, not taking his eyes off her breasts and the way they jutted out toward him, calling his name. He dropped his jeans and underwear in a heap, and quickly kicked them out of the way but slowed when he noticed Toni observing his every move.

He loved the way her gaze slid over his nakedness. The awe in her exotic brown eyes quickly turned to desire when he took his time sheathing himself as she continued to watch. Part of him wanted to just stand there, and let her eat him up with her salacious gaze, but that fantasy flew out the window when she leaned back on her arms and opened for him. *Good Lord.* His thick shaft leaped at her invitation, pulling all coherent thoughts from his brain

One step forward landed him between her thighs. "You know you can't do stuff like that and expect me to maintain any type of control."

She smiled that wicked smile of hers. "I had to do something, you were too far away. I knew a bold move would bring you to me."

She wrapped her arms around his neck and kissed him long and hard, her tongue demanding as it swept and swirled inside his mouth claiming what belonged to her. He didn't think his shaft could get any harder, but the erotic caress of her hands sliding down his back sent a shiver through his body and blood rushing to his groin. He didn't want to come across as a barbarian, but right now, all he could think about was being inside of her.

He gripped her hips hard and pulled her to the edge of the counter. A split second later, he plunged into her sweet heat and the tightness of her body that wrapped around his thickness nearly toppled him over the brink of sanity. She was his. After so many months apart, she was finally his.

"Craig," she moaned, her breath ragged against his ear, as he pumped in and out of her unable to slow his ferocious pace. She felt too good and it was as if his body was on automatic pilot. Her hands groped everywhere trying to hold on until they finally settled on his butt, drawing him even deeper inside of her.

"Ah, baby." He gritted his teeth as intense pleasure charged through his body, his thrusts in rhythm with the erratic beat of his heart. He rotated his hips and pumped faster, harder, the tip of is shaft knocking against the walls of her fiery furnace.

"Yes, yes," she panted, trying to hold on to his sweat slicked skin as he increased his pace. "Ohh, Craig," she cried. He didn't think that he would ever tire of the sexy sounds she made whenever they made love and he used everything within him to go deeper and deeper inside her. He watched as emotions distorted her beautiful face with each stroke, and his heartbeat stuttered when her muscles fastened tightly around his shaft.

"Craig!" she screamed. Her body bucked against him strong and hard, her head falling back as she gripped his arms with the strength of a person twice her size.

Watching her come with such force sent a gust of adrenaline pumping through his veins. He lifted her legs higher, and a low growl erupted from his throat as he thumped in and out of her with the speed of a locomotive, unable to slow his roll even if he wanted to.

"Toni!" he roared, his body pounding against hers with such force he could barely hold onto her as a fierce orgasm shook him to his core.

Gasping for air, they slumped against each other. Craig put most of his body weight against the counter, unsure of how long his legs would hold him up and appreciating the coolness against his skin.

"That was incredible," Toni wheezed, her forehead resting on his shoulder.

"I agree. You never cease to amaze me."

His mouth found hers and he slipped his tongue between her sweet lips, stroking and exploring the inside of her mouth. Her kiss sang through his veins, and he never wanted to let her go, never wanted to be apart from her again. For months, he had yearned to hold her in his arms, yearned to kiss her tender lips, and yearned to bury himself inside her.

He gripped the back of her head, his hands buried in her thick hair as he deepened the kiss, unable to get enough of her. Having her in his arms again was like a dream he didn't know he'd ever obtain. He didn't know what it would take, but he had every intention of making what they had together and what they just shared, permanent.

He slowly released her lips and rested his forehead against hers, placing a light kiss on the tip of her nose.

"I love you."

"I love you too." She kissed him again. "I also love quickies in the afternoon, but right now - I'm hungry. Can we eat?"

* * *

Later that evening, Craig walked into the police station to start his shift as if he had just won the lottery. The more time he spent with Toni, the more time he wanted to spend with her. Today's lunch was the best lunch he'd had in months and he was thinking about making their afternoon rendezvous a weekly event. He couldn't help chuckling to himself. Toni had already accused him of wanting her only for her body. He'd been real quick to tell her that he loved everything about her, from the way her gaze raked over him as if he were the only man on the planet, to the way she screamed his name whenever they made love. He even loved her stubbornness, at times.

"What's up detective? What are you doing here, this time of day? I thought you guys keep banker hours," Alan, a third year police officer said and glanced at his watch, "It's almost five o'clock. Time for you to be heading out the door instead of coming in."

"Well you know," Craig stroked his goatee and puffed out his chest, "being one of the big men on campus I come in whenever I want. It's all about getting the job done, no matter the time." They shared a laugh at the absurdity of Craig's statement. If they could show up whenever they wanted to, half of them would be no shows. Craig walked to his desk at the back of the room, surprised to see Floyd at his desk, which was positioned in front of Craig's.

Craig placed his coffee cup on his desk and shook out of his jacket not missing the deep worry lines across his partner's forehead. He didn't know who Floyd was talking to on the telephone, but whoever it was must have given him some bad news.

"What's up, man?" Craig asked when Floyd ended his call. "I thought you had some type of recital to attend at Charlee's school this evening." Craig sat at his desk and sipped the steaming hot coffee.

"Yeah, I do." He glanced at the clock on the wall to the right of their desks. "I have about a good hour before

I need to be out of here and heading that way if I don't want to get chewed out by my six-year-old."

Floyd and his wife of ten years had married right out of high school and had three of the cutest little girls Craig had ever seen. He didn't know if he could handle three girls and a wife, but he definitely wanted to have at least one daughter who was as cute as Toni and had her spitfire personality.

"I was about to call you." Floyd glanced around and then leaned forward, his forearms resting on his desk. "I know captain yanked us off Thomas James's case, but I thought you'd want to know what I just found out." His hoarse whisper held a hint of frustration.

Craig already knew whatever Floyd planned to tell him wasn't going to be good news. So much for walking in feeling as if he'd conquered the world. The unease swirling around in his gut told him that the rest of his day would get worse before it got better.

He sat his coffee down and leaned forward in his seat, knowing that the captain had warned them that if he found out they were still involved in the case, for any reason, he was going to suspend them.

"So what'd you find out?"

"Joyce Sanders is in the hospital in critical condition. She suffered a severe head injury, has a broken leg, cracked ribs and a punctured lung." Floyd rubbed his eyes and then looked up at Craig. "You don't even have to ask who's responsible. Two witnesses said it was her boyfriend, Thomas James."

Craig collapsed back in his seat as if someone had punched him in the gut. "Damn." He gripped the arms of his chair, trying to force air into his lungs as he willed himself to stay seated and not throw the damn chair across the room. "Please tell me they have him in custody," Craig begged. He didn't want to think about Thomas still being on the streets.

Floyd shook his head. "He's disappeared."

Anger sent a wave of heat propelling through Craig's body and he shot out of his seat, his chair rolling back and slamming into a desk. He clenched and unclenched his fist, the knot in his gut growing tighter as he paced in a circle. He ignored the curious glances. Times like this he wanted to give up his badge and go vigilante through the streets of Cincinnati. Thomas James wasn't the only bastard out there beating women, but to get even one off the streets was better than none.

Floyd stood and grabbed his bag. He eased up to Craig and said, "If you're planning to do something stupid like go after this guy, knowing that the captain pulled you off the case, call me." He gripped Craig's shoulder. "At least give me a chance to talk you out of doing something you'll regret."

CHAPTER NINE

It's days like this I hate my job. Toni stared at the opening of the two foot-by-two-foot crawl space. The entrance was larger than some, but still too narrow for most people to fit, especially since the pipe she needed to get to was at least four feet from the opening. She couldn't even pull rank and send her apprentice into the cramped space.

She unclasped her tool belt from around her waist and set it on the floor, grabbed her goggles, a stainless steel pipe clamp and a screwdriver from the belt. She checked her small flashlight to make sure the battery hadn't died, and drummed up the courage needed to enter the dark crawl space. She wasn't claustrophobic, but she didn't like tight spaces, mainly because she was terrified of rodents. Even after many years in the trades, she hadn't gotten use to seeing the vicious little critters that scared the heck out of her whenever they made an appearance.

"Are you sure there's no other way to replace the clamp or determine why the pipe is banging against the wall whenever they run the water?" Her apprentice Terrence asked. "I'm uncomfortable letting you crawl in there while I just stand around out here." He glanced at the opening and then back at her.

Always the gentleman. Instead of plumbing work, Terrence's light brown eyes, chiseled jaw, and stop-you-in-your-tracks smile could have easily landed him a modeling contract rather than an apprenticeship. Tall, buffed, with a swagger that screamed *I'm the man*, he was the vision women saw when they fantasized about hot construction workers.

Craig's concern for her safety had prompted her to hire Terrance months ago. He hated the idea of her working alone and going into a customer's house by herself, not knowing the dangers that lurked inside. At the time, she didn't want to hear his concerns, thinking that he wanted to control her. The more she thought about the safety aspect, the more she realized he had a point.

Her heart warmed at the thought of Craig. For the past four weeks, they'd spent every day together, and Toni still couldn't believe they were a couple again. They had even spent the weekend in Columbus. A ball of excitement bounced inside of her as she recalled their fun and relaxed getaway with his mother, two of his brothers and their families. It was clear that the invitation to travel with him was an expression of his intention and commitment to their future. The love his mother showed her made her wish her own parents were more demonstrative in showing love. She knew they loved her in their own special way, but sometimes...

"Toni?"

"Huh?" She shook her head when she realized she'd been caught staring off into space again, but she couldn't help daydreaming. Thoughts of Craig and her life with him raided her mind at the oddest times.

"Ah, you're thinking about the boyfriend again, huh?"

Toni lowered her head to hide the smile that wrapped her in a silken cocoon of jubilation.

"Don't be shame. When my wife and I were dating in high school, I use to sleep in my car outside her house so that I could be the first person she saw when she left for the day. I'm glad her parents liked me. Otherwise, they probably would've had me arrested for stalking." He unwrapped their extension cord and laughed a hearty laugh that would make Santa Claus's laugh sound weak.

Toni couldn't help but laugh with him.

"Okay, so back to my original question. Is there another way we can secure the pipe?"

"We could go through the wall behind the sink, but that would cost the customer more money. Since they have a crawl space, I figured we'd try this route first to save them a few bucks. If this doesn't work, then we'll go through the wall."

"All right, I guess we should get started."

Toni made quick work of replacing the clamp that had pulled away from the wall, and then crawled in a little farther to tighten a screw that had also pulled away from the wall. Between the cobwebs and the dust, she couldn't get out of there fast enough. She wiped the perspiration from her forehead with the back of her hand and blew out an exaggerated breath. *It's days like this I definitely hate my job. Maybe we should have gone through the wall. At least then, I wouldn't be sweating like I just ran a marathon.*

She shined her flashlight along the length of the wall and stopped when she noticed another screw hanging from a clamp. It was no wonder the pipe was knocking around every time they ran the faucet. There was nothing keeping it in place.

She laid the flashlight down and picked up her screwdriver, but froze. A spine-tingling sensation skittered down her back. Sharp claws scratching against plaster sent her heart rate from sixty to a thousand within seconds, and her gaze frantically darted around the tight space trying to find the source of the noise. *Okay, don't panic. It might be nothing.* As soon as the thought was complete a small ball of fur zoomed past her outstretched arm.

"Aarrghhh!"

A scream flew through her lips, and panic shattered the confidence that she'd built up before entering the space. She bolted upright and banged her head on a steel pipe. A stabbing sensation shot through her head and tears stung her eyes. Twinkling stars clouded her vision as nausea rolled around in her stomach and worked its way up to her throat. *Oh God help me.* She fought hard to keep the swell of bile from spilling out of her mouth, but the unbearable pounding in her head, she couldn't control.

"Toni, what's happening in there?" Terrence called out, his voice frantic. "Toni!"

Her eyelids grew heavier and heavier, Terrence's voice faded further and further into the background.

"Help," she rasped. Her mouth opened to say more, but no words came out. Instead, darkness descended upon her and pulled her under.

***

Craig hurried through the doors of the hospital, panic rioting through his body as he glanced around the area in search of an information desk.

"Toni has been rushed to emergency," Peyton had told him. Her words thereafter were blurred by the crazy thoughts racing through his mind. He immediately thought the worse until she forced him to listen and assured him that Toni was going to be fine, but he wouldn't be satisfied until he saw her for himself.

"Excuse me," he said to the blond with shocking blue eyes sitting behind the counter. "I'm looking for Toni Jenkins. She was brought into emergency about an hour ago."

The receptionist typed something into the computer and glanced back at him. "And you are?"

He flashed his badge. "Detective Craig Logan. It's imperative that I speak with her." What good was a police badge if he couldn't use it for moments like this?

Seconds later Craig was heading in the direction that the receptionist had told him, remembering all the reasons why he hated Toni's job. He probably hated her job more than she hated his. Why couldn't she be a secretary or a computer programmer, something that wouldn't be physically detrimental to her health? She could easily use her engineering degree and get an office job, but no, she had to work in construction, risking her life unnecessarily every day.

Craig came to a halt once he reached the area the receptionist directed him to. There were four small areas with beds sectioned off by heavy curtains. He was told that Toni's bed was behind the last curtain.

Craig almost laughed at himself when he realized he was holding his breath, unease froze his feet and kept him at the entrance of the space. One would think he didn't see blood and injured people on a daily basis, but the thought of his woman being hurt was totally different. She meant everything to him and he had to still himself from the anxiousness brewing in his gut.

He eased to the rear of the room, surprised Toni's family or at least her cousins weren't still there. He stopped and stood several feet from her, his heart pounding hard in his chest. Long eyelashes that rested against her high cheekbones flew up as if she had sensed his presence.

"Craig," she whispered, her usual bright smile vacant from her lips.

He studied her, taking in the dark circles around her eyes and the large bandage on the right side of her forehead. He didn't know the full details of what happened, but he was thankful she was all right.

"You scared me to death," he finally spoke. What he really wanted to do was to scoop her up into his arms and hold her tight, but she looked so fragile. He kissed her lips and moved her hair away from her face. "Are you okay?"

"Yes," she hesitated. "Who called you? This wasn't that serious, I just bumped my head."

"Anytime you're hurt or in pain is serious to me," he choked out, his shaky voice betrayed the calm facade he tried to present. "I called your cell phone and Peyton answered. Besides the slight concussion and the gash near your temple, are you hurt anywhere else? You look as if you did more than bump your head." He sat on the side of the bed and lifted her hand to his lips, kissing the inside of her wrist.

"I'm all right, but my head hurts and I want to go to sleep."

"Well, it looked as if you were asleep when I walked in."

"Martina, Peyton and Christina left a few minutes ago. I was resting my eyes for a minute." She started to rub her head but halted her hand mid-air as if suddenly remembering she had a bandage there. "The doctor doesn't want me to sleep yet because I was dizzy and had trouble walking."

"What?" Craig stiffened suddenly concerned that Peyton hadn't told him everything. He glanced over Toni's body and zoned in on her legs. "Why were you dizzy? Did you fall or something? What happened exactly?" His heart rate kicked up, afraid of what she'd say next.

She closed her eyes and lightly moved her head from side to side. "Craig, I feel so stupid."

"You and I both know you're not stupid. Tell me what happened." He attempted to stand, but she held his hand tight, forced him to stay where he was.

After hesitating, she spoke. "I was reattaching a pipe to a wall inside a tight crawl space and heard a noise. I … I froze." She opened her eyes and tears rolled down her face. Craig held her hand tighter, encouraging her to keep going with her story. "I thought I heard something, and then I … I saw a mouse." She shivered. "Just thinking about mice creeps me out."

He moved closer and kissed her lips, wiping her tears in the process. "Come on, baby, don't cry. You're here and you're safe. That's all that matters right now."

He knew she was deathly afraid of rodents. He had gained that bit of knowledge first hand when he hired

Jenkins & Sons to do some plumbing work at his house and Toni showed up. Once he got over the initial shock of her being a real plumber, he hired her to fix the issue with an upstairs toilet and a pipe that ran into the basement. Unfortunately, while in the basement, she crossed paths with a squirrel and totally fell apart. He'd never forget the fear he felt when he walked into the house and heard her crying and screaming, only to find her in the basement standing on top of his dryer. That moment led to them falling into to bed and making love. He'd been madly in love with her ever since.

"You know I can't handle it when you cry," he whispered and kissed her cheek.

"I know," she mumbled, trying to pull herself together. "I'm sorry. I know it seems stupid to cry over seeing a rodent, but I just can't help it."

As Craig continued to wipe her tears, he wondered if bumping her head caused her to pass out or if it were from her phobia.

"Hey Toni, it looks like ..." Terrence's words died mid-sentence when he walked into the tight space and saw Craig. "Oh, I'm sorry. I didn't realize you had a visitor."

"Who the hell are you?" Craig rose slowly wondering why some pretty boy was bringing his woman flowers. "And why are you just walking in here as if you belong?"

"Down boy," Toni joked quietly and wiped the rest of her tears away. She lifted her upper body but grabbed her head suddenly. "Oh God," she groaned, her voice hollow from the lightning bolt of pain that pierced her skull. She gritted her teeth, braced on her elbows and eased gently back onto the pillow, inhaling and exhaling slowly to steady her erratic breathing.

His stomach lurched. Craig couldn't stand seeing her in pain. Brows furrowed, with the back of his hand, he stroked her cheek. "I'm going to get the doctor." He turned to leave and his glare shot daggers at Terrence.

"Craig, don't. No more doctors. I just need to lie still for awhile." She closed her eyes for a few seconds and then met his gaze. "Oh, and that's Terrence, my apprentice."

Craig stared at her for a moment to determine if she were serious, then he glanced at Terrence. *Her apprentice? When in the heck did she get an apprentice?*

"I thought apprentices were usually in their early twenties. You're a little old aren't you?" The jagged barb meant to wipe the smug look off pretty boy's face didn't seem to faze him.

"Craig!" Toni gasped. "I can't believe you asked him that. Apprentices can be any age as long as they can do the work," she spat out, her stern gaze drilled into him.

Terrence chuckled and sat the flowers down on the small table next to the bed. "It's all right, Toni. I get that a lot. As a matter of fact," he said to Craig, "my *wife* jokes about my choice of career at this age all the time."

Craig glanced at Toni. She no longer pierced him with her disapproving glare. Instead, he saw humor in her eyes and a self-satisfied expression on her face. It served him right for being jealous that she worked with someone who looked as if he should be on the cover of Super Model Today.

"Craig, nice to meet you finally." Terrence extended his hand, and they shook. "Toni, I'll catch you tomorrow. Get some rest."

SHARON C. COOPER

Toni waited until Terrence left before she spoke. "Sometimes I like that you're protective of me, but this jealousy stuff has to stop."

Craig shrugged unfazed by her reprimand and reclaimed his position next to her. "Hey, what can I say? Old habits die hard."

"Just because you find me totally irresistible, doesn't mean every other man does." She intertwined her fingers with his and he found comfort in having her close.

"Nah, baby. Any red-blooded man who lays eyes on you probably finds you extremely attractive. I know this because I see the looks you get when we're out together, and it doesn't seem to matter that I'm standing right next to you. So forgive me if I turn a little green when some guy is eyeing you. By the way, what did he mean by 'I'll see you tomorrow?' I know you're not planning to go back to work tomorrow."

"Actually I was planning on going back to work, but the doctor suggested I take a couple of days off. At first, I wasn't planning to listen, but I feel like crap." She released a ragged sigh. "So I'll do as recommended."

"Good, because I'd hate to have to handcuff you to the bedpost. Then again, that might not be such a bad idea."

CHAPTER TEN

Toni stared out the passenger window as Craig drove to her grandparents' house for Sunday brunch. Like most African American families, they came together weekly to eat, laugh and for the occasional argument. Toni immediately thought of Martina. Despite the family's closeness, her cousin was good at getting everyone riled up. It was always something with her. Whether the topics were social, family, or lately political issues, MJ found a way to turn every discussion into an argument. At times, it seemed she lived to argue, but when she wasn't stirring up trouble, Martina was as loyal and devoted to the family as any of the Jenkins.

"You're awfully quiet," Craig said breaking into her thoughts. He reached for her hand and squeezed it. "Are you feeling okay?"

Her heart flipped at the genuine concern in his voice and the love that glittered in his eyes when he glanced at her. She lifted their joined hands up to her mouth and kissed the back of his. From the day he carried her home from the hospital, he'd been watching her every move, making sure she wanted for nothing.

"I'm fine. I was just thinking about the brunch."

"What about the brunch? Are you having second thoughts about me tagging along?"

"Definitely not." She turned in her seat to face him. "You know my family loves you. I was just thinking about MJ. I hope she doesn't show her tail this afternoon."

Craig laughed. "Yeah, she is a trip. I've never known anyone to speak their mind quite the way she does."

"I know, right?" Toni shook her head. "I missed brunch last Sunday, but lately she has been on this political kick. She's always been active with the carpenters union, and now that the governor is trying to strip union workers of their collective bargaining rights, oh my goodness, she has become downright evil. I mean I agree that we need to fight this, but she has taken her anger over the idea to an entirely different level."

Craig shuddered. "Whew, I would hate to be a politician and have to come face to face with her."

"I know I hope she never meets Senator Paul Kendrick face to face. He's really pushing for change, and though she's never met the guy, she can't stand him. I'm wondering if I or another family member should warn his office. Let them know to stay clear of Martina MJ Jenkins." They both laughed, but the more Toni thought about the idea, the more she thought that maybe she should reach out to the senator.

They were both still laughing when Craig pulled into her grandparent's driveway. Toni's face heated when she thought about the last time she and Craig were both at her grandparent's home, and that toe-curling kiss they shared near the back door.

"Looks like everyone is already here." Craig opened the car door for her. "You guys don't have a tradition that who's ever the last one to arrive has to wash the dishes afterwards do you?"

"Ha! No and don't give my grandmother any ideas."

They walked around to the back of the house and Toni was surprised to see everything set up in the back yard. It was a nice May afternoon, but as far as she was concerned, it was still a little chilly outside.

"Well, look who decided to make an appearance." Martina walked out of the house carrying two chafer pans. "Officer Logan, glad you decided to join us. It was starting to get a little boring around here for me. I'm running out of people to pick on."

"What's up, MJ?" They hugged, and Craig stepped back. "Glad to see you're still giving everyone a hard time. I wore my thick skin today, so bring your best game."

"Oh, please. Don't get her started," Christina, Toni's cousin and Peyton's younger sister said when she walked out of the house with a large pitcher of water for the chafer pans. "We're already thinking about kicking her out of the family."

Before she headed back into the house, Martina's middle finger shot up in an obscene gesture, leaving the three of them laughing.

"It's been a long time, Officer Logan." Christina stuck her arm through his and then whispered in his ear. "I'm glad you and TJ are back together. I'm pulling for you guys."

Craig smiled down at her. "Thank you, I appreciate that. I'm giving it my best shot."

"Hey, don't you know it's impolite to whisper in front of someone?" Toni grabbed hold of Craig's other arm and narrowed her eyes playfully at her cousin. "Anyway, I don't know why you're whispering, he's just going to tell me what you said later."

"Ohh, Cuz, do you feel left out?" Christina threw her arm around Toni's shoulder. "I only told him that he's a very lucky man to have you in his life."

"Aw, that's so sweet." Toni wrapped her arms around Christina's mid-section. "Feel free to whisper in his ear anytime if you're going to say things like that."

Christina (CJ) Jenkins was one of Toni's favorite cousins. They were only a year apart and grew up as sisters more so than cousins. As adults, they didn't see each other as often as Toni would like, especially since lately Christina traveled a lot, but Toni knew she always could count on CJ if she needed to.

"CJ, I forgot to ask you, how did the mural for the community center turn out?" Toni asked. "I heard you finished painting it yesterday."

Christina, the painter in the family, had been commissioned by *Never too Old to Learn Community Center* to paint a mural in the front entrance of their new building.

"Not to sound conceited, but I think the project was some of my best work to date."

The three of them talked for a few minutes longer before Craig and Toni made their rounds to speak to everyone. As Toni expected, her family was glad to see her and Craig back together.

"Toni, sweetheart, can you come in and give me a hand with something?" Her grandmother beckoned her from the doorway.

"Are you going to be okay out here by yourself?" Toni asked Craig.

"Of course." He pulled her in his arms and kissed her, not caring who witnessed the intimate exchange. "But hurry back, I'm a little afraid. Your cousin MJ has been eyeing me and I'm sure she's planning to make me her next victim."

Toni laughed and headed into the kitchen where her grandmother flitted about adding the finishing touches to a few dishes.

"Hey, Gram, what can I help with?" Toni washed and dried her hands. "It looks like you outdid yourself today. Everything smells wonderful."

"You know this is what I live for, cooking for my family." She patted Toni on the cheek and placed a kiss on her forehead. "How are you feeling? Are you still having those headaches?

"A few here and there, but I'll live." She placed her hands palms down on the counter and eyed the chocolate cake her grandmother was frosting. "What can I do to help? Do you need me to taste the cake for you?" Toni asked, trying to maintain a straight face, but her grandmother didn't miss the twitch at the corners of her lips.

"Don't even think about it," she threatened, waving her white plastic spatula at Toni. "Instead of eyeing my cake, grab the two salads from the refrigerator."

Unlike many people of her grandparent's wealth, her grandmother insisted on being the one to cook for her family. Years ago, before her grandfather retired, he wanted to hire a housekeeper to take care of the cooking and the household cleaning. Her grandmother nixed the idea claiming she cooked and cleaned when they were eating pork n beans and spam. Now that they were living up on the hill, things would be no different. The only time they hired help was when they had a huge event that included people outside of the family.

"Should I grab this vegetable tray too?" She pointed at the round tray that took up most of the second shelf in the doublewide refrigerator.

"Oh, I forgot about that. I'll need you to add a few more carrots and cucumbers first. I saw your dad and your uncle Marty eating from it earlier."

"It looks like they scarfed down most of the tomatoes too."

Her grandmother shook her head. "Those boys. They never can wait until we set everything out."

They worked together in companionable silence. After a few minutes her grandmother said, "I'm glad to see your young man here with you today."

Toni smiled to herself. "Me too."

"I can tell you're happier than you've been in awhile. I can't help but think that Craig has something to do with that glow brightening up your beautiful face."

Toni leaned against the counter. Her eyes gazed heavenward and she sighed wearing a goofy grin on her face. "He makes me feel … like, like … oh I don't know, like I'm the most important person in the world. He's always doing things for me, little things. He probably doesn't even know how special those little things are to me." She poured the bag of carrots into a strainer and rinsed them.

"I know what you mean," her grandmother chuckled. "When your grandpa was courting me," she paused, "or as you young people say today, trying to date me, he did a lot of little things too. Like when he used to drive across town to pick me up from high school during my junior year so that I wouldn't have to walk. Mind you, I only lived two blocks from the school."

Her grandmother laughed and Toni couldn't help but smile. She loved hearing stories about when her grandparents dated.

"Is that when you knew he was the one?" Toni asked.

Her grandmother propped her hip against the counter and took a moment to think. "No, I think it was when I was suspended from school."

Toni's mouth dropped opened. "Whaaat, you were suspended from school? Gramma I can't believe it." Her grandmother was petite, almost prissy-like. Toni couldn't imagine her doing anything wrong. "How? Why?"

Her grandmother giggled like a schoolgirl at Toni's shock. "I wasn't always a goodie-two-shoe. Like you, I had those moments when I had to ask myself, 'What were you thinking?' Of course, I always asked after the fact." She laughed good-naturedly.

"Okay, so why'd you get suspended."

"Smoking in the girl's bathroom. Twice!"

"What? You used to smoke!" Toni set the vegetables down and dried her hands. "Oh, man, wait until I tell—"

"And if you do," she threatened with her spatula again, "you'll never get another lick of my peach cobbler - ever."

Without hesitation Toni said, "My lips are sealed.

"Well anyway, I knew your grandfather was the one when I called him at his job to tell him what happened, and he left work immediately to come and take me out to lunch."

That's it? Toni thought to herself. She expected her grandmother to say something a lot grander than *he took me out to lunch.*

"There was no condemnation, no judgment, nothing. I don't even think he would have asked for details had I not brought up the subject. Once I told him what happened, he asked if I wanted him to go home with me to be there when I told my parents." Her grandmother smiled and went back to frosting the cake. "I knew then that I would spend the rest of my life with that man."

Toni threw her arms around her grandmother's shoulder. "You guys are the best. I'm so glad you chose each other. I can't imagine my life without either of you."

"Actually, dear," she bumped Toni with her hip, "you wouldn't have a life without either of us. How do you think you would've gotten here if we hadn't gotten together?"

Toni laughed and shook her head at her grandmother. At seventy-two, she still had a wickedly funny sense of humor.

"Now tell me what's going on with you and that handsome police officer."

Toni filled her in on what they'd been up to for the past few weeks, less the sexcapades.

"So do you think he's the one?"

Toni didn't have to think twice. "Yes."

"Then what's stopping you from marrying him?"

Toni's eyes bulged. "How did you know he asked me?"

"I didn't know until just now." She smiled and winked.

Toni's mouth dropped opened. "Gramma, you scare me sometimes. I didn't know you were so devious!"

"I raised four sons, and three daughters. I had to be a step ahead in order to keep up with what was going on." She set a second cake on the counter and began to spread frosting over the top. "So what are you waiting for? Why haven't you accepted his proposal?"

"He asked me before we broke up. He hasn't asked since then. Besides, even if he did ask again, I don't know if I can be what he wants, or needs me to be."

Silence filled the kitchen. Toni thought about her statement and knew that at some point soon, she was going to have a long talk with Craig.

"I've seen the way he looks at you," her grandmother spoke in her usual gentle tone. "He loves you for who you are good or bad. The person *you* decide to spend your life with should be a person who understands that you're not perfect, but they love you anyway."

Toni placed plastic wrap over the vegetable trays and a clear cake cover over one of the cakes while her grandmother talked. It had been a long time since she and her grandmother had a one-on-one, something they use to have often before Toni went off to college. Something that Toni missed more than she realized.

"Chile, there are things that I've said and done that I know pushed your grandfather's love for me to his limits." Her gentle laugh rippled through the air, "but I know he loves me anyway. He accepts my imperfections and at times, my poor judgment. So don't think that you can't give Craig what he wants or what he needs. By the sparkle in his eyes whenever he looks at you, he knows you're the one to fulfill his every desire."

SHARON C. COOPER

Toni hoped her grandmother was right. Now that she and Craig had found their way back to each other, she didn't want to go back to living life without him. This made the conversation she knew she had to have with him, that much harder to consider.

***

Craig watched from his position near the pool as the Jenkins women cleared the serving dishes and carried them inside the house. He tuned out the conversations around him, finding himself too distracted by Toni. Her laugh, the way she interacted with her family, and her killer body. He knew oh too well what lie beneath that soft, yellow T-shirt she wore, full voluptuous breasts that made his mouth water and his hands itch in anticipation whenever they were disrobed. But it wasn't just her sexiness, it was the total package. She was perfectly flawed. Her penchant for finding trouble, quick temper, and her rodent phobia were a few of her imperfections, yet, as far as he was concerned, she was perfect for him.

"You haven't taken your eyes off her since you arrived," the deep baritone voice said from behind him.

Craig glanced over his shoulder to find Steven Jenkins pulling up a chair next to his, under the large red and blue table umbrella. Craig stood to move his chair over, but Mr. Jenkins stopped him.

"Oh you're fine. I figured I'd just come over and sit a spell since I haven't had a chance to talk with you. Did you enjoy the brunch?"

"Definitely. Your wife's cooking is as good as I remember." He rubbed his stomach recalling the peach cobbler he'd just scarfed down.

"If that's the case, why is this my first time seeing you in months?"

Craig knew Toni's grandfather was aware of their separation so he could only assume he was talking about the last few weeks since he and Toni had reunited.

"Well, sir, I usually have to work on Sundays. This is the first Sunday I've had off in months."

Steven Jenkins shook his head. "It's a shame folks have to work on Sundays. Back in my day, Sundays were the one day where you attended church and then rested. But I guess working for the police department makes that kind of impossible."

"Yes sir. Unfortunately, we don't always have the luxury of weekends and holidays off."

"Well, you definitely have an honorable job, and I have the utmost respect for what you and your colleagues do."

"Thank you, sir."

They sat in a comfortable silence, despite the chattering all around them. Craig looked up in time to see Toni walking toward him until her mother stopped her. He wasn't sure what was said, but they both walked into the house along with a couple of other women.

"I'm glad to see you two back together," Toni's grandfather interrupted his thoughts. "My granddaughter was a different person when you weren't around. I saw changes in her I didn't like, but as a grandparent, sometimes you have to sit back and let your children find their own way."

Craig glanced toward the door that Toni had entered. "There wasn't a day that went by that I didn't think about her," he said more to himself than to her grandfather.

"I can tell you're in love with her. I see a special tenderness in the way you look at her and the way you treat her as if she's a precious piece of fine china."

Craig turned to her grandfather. "She's very important to me. And you're right. I'm very much in love with her."

"Well, I'm sure the reason you haven't married her then is because she's too damn stubborn."

Craig laughed but didn't confirm the comment.

"You don't have to agree with me. I know. We practically raised that girl when her parents were going through a rough patch a year or two after she was born. As she grew older, she spent more time with Katherine and me than she did at home. From day one TJ had me wrapped around her finger, and as she grew older, the wrap became tighter." He laughed a hearty laugh. "Once she became a teen, I finally realized why my relationship with her has always been a little different than the relationships I have with my other granddaughters."

"And what was that?" Craig had noticed early on that there was a special relationship between Toni and her grandfather. Even her cousins teased her about being their grandfather's favorite, despite the fact that he clearly adored all of his granddaughters.

"She reminds me of her grandmother. When I first met Katherine, she gave me all kind of hell." He shook his head and smiled as if remembering some special moments. "But I can't imagine my life without her. She used to get into all types of trouble. She has spunk and is ridiculously independent, and she is one of the most loving people I have ever met in my life. Toni is so much like her."

Craig listened as Toni's grandfather shared tales of when he and his beloved Katherine dated, as well as some of the challenges they faced early in their marriage.

"Mr. Jenkins, how did you do it – stay happily married for over fifty years?"

He chuckled and scratched his head. "Son, I often ask myself the same question. But I think Katherine would agree that one of the most important things we do is work at our marriage every day. We spend as much time together as we can, kissing, hugging or whatever it takes to keep the love we have for each other alive. And most importantly, we're quick to forgive and quick to say I'm sorry."

Craig bobbed his head in understanding, appreciating the wisdom of Toni's grandfather and taking in his words.

"So does this mean you're thinking about marriage?"

"I've been thinking about marriage since the day I met Toni. I'm very much in love with your granddaughter, and I plan to ask her to marry me … again."

CHAPTER ELEVEN

"What's up, man?" Derek said in a rush when he opened the door for Craig and Toni, the cordless phone against his chest. "You guys come on in. I need to finish up this call real quick." He hurried back down the hall toward his office not giving Craig a chance to respond.

"Hey, Uncle Craig!" Jason, Craig's three-year-old nephew, stormed down the hallway and leaped into his arms. "Did you come over to watch a movie with me? How about *Toy Story 2*, your favorite?"

A hearty laugh spilled from Craig's gut and he immediately felt some of the day's tension fall away. "What's up li'l man? I actually came over to talk with your dad, but I guess we can watch a movie. Hold up, haven't we watched *Toy Story 2* like a thousand times?"

"Yes," he said, his head moving up and down like a bobble-head toy. "But it's your favorite."

That got another chuckle out of Craig before his brother walked up and gave him a fist bump. "Sorry about that. I've been waiting all day to hear from the project manager of this new assignment and of course she calls right when the doorbell rings." Derek picked up two pairs of Jason's shoes that were sitting in the middle of the foyer. "Where's Toni?"

"She's standing outside finishing up a call."

"Auntie Toni's here?" Jason asked, his eyes round with surprise. "I'll go get her." He squirmed in Craig's arms, but Craig didn't let him down.

"Hold on li'l man. She'll be in shortly."

"Jason, I told you hours ago to take these shoes to your room. Instead of you trying to get outside, I want you to put them up, now." Craig sat Jason on his feet and watched as his nephew shoved the little race car he was holding into his pocket before he grabbed his shoes.

"I'll be back Uncle Craig."

"Li'l man, when you're finished putting your shoes away, why don't you go ahead and set up the movie. Auntie Toni and I will be in there in a few minutes. Okay?"

"Okay." Jason took off running down the hall.

"Sometimes I wonder if he knows how to walk since he runs everywhere," Derek said shaking his head. "I better go make sure he doesn't just toss the shoes in the middle of the floor of his bedroom. Come on back to the family room when Toni finishes up."

Craig glanced out the door. Toni paced the concrete stoop, and when her eyes met his, she lifted a finger and mouthed *one minute*. Craig nodded. The past few weeks with her were like old times: they ate together, re-incorporated their Friday date nights and did practically everything together outside of working hours. A flutter of excitement swelled in his stomach. They were officially a couple. She was his and he was hers. Finally.

SHARON C. COOPER

Seconds later, Toni entered. "I'm so sorry, that was Peyton. On Friday, we're having a girls night out to celebrate Jada finishing her apprenticeship. She wanted to get my vote on where we should meet."

"No problem." He grabbed hold of her hand and locked the door. "I didn't want to leave you by yourself."

She shook her head. "You're doing it again."

"Doing what?" He hunched his shoulders, his brows furrowed.

"Being over protective. You didn't have to wait for me. I would've come in once I was done."

Craig ran his hand over his head and down the back of his neck. This was an ongoing discussion between them and she claimed that he'd gotten worse since her accident. He glanced down at her and his heart swelled with all the love he had for her. Sure, he might be a little overprotective but it was because he was crazy about her.

"I know you can take care of yourself, but I felt waiting on you would be the gentleman thing to do." After the day he'd had, he definitely didn't feel like arguing.

"You're such a sweetheart. You always know the right thing to say." She wrapped her arms around him and stood on her tiptoes for a kiss. "I'm sorry for making a big deal over nothing."

"And I promise to chill a bit. It's hard though. You mean everything to me, so forgive me for being a little overprotective."

He claimed Toni's mouth and crushed her to him, her lips soft and tender. He didn't think he would ever get accustomed to having her in his arms, being able to hold and love on her. It was as if he could breathe again.

"All right you two. There's a minor in the house," Derek said from the end of the hall carrying a bowl of popcorn. "Either grab one of the guest rooms upstairs or chill with that stuff."

Craig chuckled and wrapped his arm around Toni's shoulder. "Yes sir, we'll be good. Then again, maybe we should test out one of your beds upstairs."

Toni swatted his arm. "Stop." She giggled and leaned into Craig. "Derek, we'll be good."

***

Toni stood near the opening to Derek's family room watching Jason as he sang and danced along to the movie he was watching. He was the cutest kid ever, but he was also a reminder of what she would never have.

"Auntie Toni!" Jason screamed when he saw her. His tiny legs shot across the family room and charged toward Toni at full speed.

"Whoa, li'l man!" Craig scooped him up before he reached her. "Slow down, dude. Auntie Toni was released from the hospital a few days ago. You can give her a hug, but you can't jump on her. Got it?"

"Got it," Jason slapped his uncle a big boy high five."

"Craig?" Toni lifted her arms and let them fall back down. "What are you doing? It's been almost a week. I'm fine."

"No, you're not. Your balance is still off." He challenged, his gaze boring into hers with the intensity of the sun blazing over a blacktop roof. "Don't think I haven't noticed."

Toni cocked her head and her mouth gaped open, surprised by his words. Yes, she still had daily headaches and some days the light-headedness made her feel as if she'd throw up if she moved too fast. What shocked her, though, was that Craig had noticed.

With Jason in his arms, Craig stepped closer to her. "I notice everything about you," he whispered next to her ear, sending a delicious tingle up her spine. He allowed Jason to lean in and give her a hug.

Toni didn't speak. Instead, she wrapped her arms around Jason and kissed him on the cheek, but her eyes stayed locked on Craig. She didn't think she could ever love him as much as she did at that moment. Her protector. That's what he was, always taking care of her even when she wasn't aware.

"I love you," she mouthed the words over Jason's head. He winked and blew her a kiss.

"Auntie Toni." Jason leaned back to look at her, his small arm barely making it around her neck. "You're my girlfriend too." He kissed her on the cheek. His soft lips brought tears to her eyes, and she knew that even the younger Logan man was going to be a heartbreaker.

"Aww," Toni cooed and turned to plant a kiss on his forehead.

"Aww, nothing," Craig yanked Jason away before her lips made contact. "Man, what you doin'?" He jokingly chastised his nephew. "She's my girlfriend, and you need to go and find your own girlfriend."

"No, she's my girlfriend," Jason giggled as Craig tickled him, turned him upside down and held him by his legs. "Daddy! Help me! Daddy!"

"Craig, be careful. You're going to hurt him. You're being too rough," Toni said but couldn't help but laugh along with them. Jason was the type of kid you couldn't help but fall in love with. Smart, funny and an absolute cutie-pie just like his uncle.

Toni jumped and her hand flew to her chest when Craig dipped Jason so low that it seemed he would hit his head on the floor. "Craig, be careful!" She lunged toward them planning to pull Jason out of his arms, but Craig turned his body.

"Hey, hey, hey, what you doin' to my son?" Derek playfully punched Craig in the arm, and Jason threw his head back and laughed harder.

"He's trying to steal my girlfriend, and you know I can't have that." Craig pretended to punch Jason in the stomach over and over again, throwing out grunts to add to the playful moment.

Toni watched the three of them tussle around on the sofa and then the floor. As a single dad, Derek was awesome, and there was no doubt he loved his son. He was a great father and Toni knew Craig would be too.

A sudden bout of sadness swept through her when she thought about not being able to give Craig what he wanted the most, a family. For weeks, she had put off talking to him. Instead she was living for the moment, loving the attention and the love he gave freely, when what she needed to do was tell him her main reason for walking away from him months ago. She needed to tell him she couldn't have children.

***

"I feel like I'm obsessed with her," Craig said and paced in front of Derek's desk. Since Jason insisted on watching the second movie with just Toni, it gave Craig and Derek a chance to visit. "This feeling of always wanting to be in Toni's presence, always wanting to hear her laugh or see her smile. Am I crazy?"

"Probably," Derek joked but sobered when Craig narrowed his eyes at him. "Hey, I'm no psychiatrist. Do you feel like you're crazy?"

Craig thought for a moment. "No, I seriously feel as if I'm obsessed. Some days are worse than others. One minute I'm afraid to let her walk out the door alone because I know the craziness that walks the streets of Cincinnati and then the next minute I just want to be near her, to hold her close and never let her go again."

His brother leaned back in his office chair and studied Craig before saying, "Yeah you do sound a little obsessive, but you also sound like a man who is very much in love with his woman. I think part of the obsessiveness has to do with your job and your need to free the world of abusive men."

Craig couldn't argue with Derek's assessment, but he didn't know how to fix the problem. It was easy to say that he would back off and try not to suffocate Toni with the love he felt for her, but it was another thing to actually back off.

Silence fell between them and Craig heard his nephew in the other room singing along with the Disney movie he and Toni were watching. He'd kill to be young and carefree again. Instead, he was working at a job that stressed him out, while trying to save the city from scumbags. And if that were not enough, he couldn't stop thinking about the woman he was crazy in love with.

Craig stood near Derek's desk and picked up one of Jason's racing cars, spinning the tiny button-size wheels. "You're definitely right about my obsession with ridding the world of people like that idiot I told you about last week. When I found out he beat his ex so bad that she ended up hospitalized, I wanted to turn in my badge and gun. I wanted to hunt him down like the dirty dog he is," he spat out. His gut churned with the same nauseous bitterness he felt right after Floyd told him about Joyce Sander's attack. "The woman could have helped if she hadn't recanted her story, but that's beside the point. We need tougher laws to keep these guys locked up." He set the car back on the desk and rubbed his forehead with both hands before dropping them to his side. "These types of cases always get to me, but this one in particular has me losing sleep."

"So what has you more upset, being pulled off the case or that this man has gone free?"

"Does it matter? Both situations are messed up."

"Craig, maybe you need to take some time off." His brother rose from his seat and placed his hands, palms down, on the desk. "I know how deep you get into cases of domestic violence, and you said yourself that lately most of the crimes you've been investigating are crimes against women." He walked around the desk and stood next to Craig, his hands shoved into his pants pockets. "Your captain knows what you've been through, first Cynthia's death and then Julien's. I know you're trying to save the world, or at least women, but even you, Detective Extraordinaire, need a break sometime."

"I know. You're right." He hadn't had a vacation all year and was way overdue for some down time.

"And what about the other situation?"

"What other situation?"

"The situation that has you smothering your woman. You know as well as I do Toni is not going to stand for you hovering over her all the time." He held up his hand when Craig began to protest. "Hear me out. She's a tough, independent woman who took care of herself just fine before you came along."

Craig moved to the window and stared out into the night, looking at nothing in particular. He heard his brother's words, but his brother didn't have all the facts. He didn't know Toni had been raped while in college, brutalized by someone who might still be walking the streets. Craig never wanted her to experience that type of emotional or physical pain again. No woman should go through that type of violation.

"There's something else you need to think about," Derek said from across the room.

Craig glanced over his shoulder. "And what's that?"

"If you keep smothering her, you're going to risk losing her again. You're going to have to give her some space."

Craig turned back to the window. "I know, I know … and I will," he said in annoyance. He rubbed his forehead again to relieve the dull ache that was slowly building. He definitely didn't want to lose Toni.

"One more thing, now that you and Toni are back together, what are you going to do about Patricia?"

CHAPTER TWELVE

Craig pulled up to the Kingsgate Marriott hotel and handed his keys to the valet. Up until a couple of months ago, he'd been spending at least one weekend a month here and was glad to say that he wouldn't miss the visits, but he would miss Patricia Edison.

He met Patricia years ago while vacationing in Vegas. They hit it off immediately and tried a long distance relationship for months, him living in Cincinnati and her living in Chicago, but soon realized long distance romance was too much. Though they cared for each other, neither was ready or willing to make the sacrifice of leaving their cities or careers. But when Patricia called him, a month after he and Toni split, they picked up where they left off, she visited Cincinnati as often as she could visit, and he made several trips to Chicago.

He stood in the hallway outside of Patricia's hotel room door. Regret crawled up his spine as he stared at the room number plate embossed in gold, sick about the conversation that he was getting ready to have. One last glance down the brightly lit hall and then he knocked. Within seconds, the door swung open, and he wasn't surprised to see her in the skimpy lingerie. He gave her tight, curvy body an appreciative once over, before returning his gaze to her face. There was a time when his body would respond immediately, but not this time. Since Toni had walked back into his life, no other woman made his body come alive the way Toni did.

"Hey, boo, what took you so long to get here?" Her Chicago accent was more prominent than he remembered.

Craig stepped across the threshold and knew this conversation was going to be harder than he originally thought. He cared about Patricia, but he was in love with Toni.

"What? No kiss, no hug, no squeeze?" Patricia closed the door and turned to Craig. "What's going on?" Her hands cocked on her hip, the thin lace material stretched across her ample breasts tempted him with her taut nipples.

Craig blew out a breath. The longer she stood in front of him with her skimpy outfit, the more his pulse picked up speed. He glanced around the room before looking back at her. "We need to talk."

Her eyes narrowed and the welcoming smile she had when she first opened the door slipped from her lips. Shoulders suddenly drooped, she clamped her arms across her perky breasts and held herself in a tight grip.

"What do you want to talk about?" A nervous tremble rattled her words.

Craig ran a hand slowly over his head and down the back of his neck before dropping his arm to his side. He stared at her without speaking. Her bronze toned skin glistened, and those large expressive eyes stared back at him waiting for him to say something, anything. What could he say? She was a beautiful woman on the outside whose personality made her just as beautiful inside. Intelligent, but serious, she was submissive, agreeable, and a neat freak … everything Toni wasn't.

"We need to talk about us," he finally said. "But first why don't you go and get dressed."

"Craig." She shifted her weight to one hip, her eyes pleading.

"Please." He nodded his head toward her bedroom door and wondered what he'd gotten himself into.

She opened her mouth to speak, but nothing came out. Craig didn't miss the battle waging inside her. Part of her probably wanted to argue, but he knew she wouldn't. Arguing wasn't her style. She studied him for a few moments longer and then slunk off to the bedroom of the suite.

Craig moved to the large wall-to-wall windows and stared out into the night, taking in the view of building rooftops and the busy streets below. Patricia knew of Toni, but not that he and Toni had reunited.

A twinge of guilt knotted his stomach. He had too much respect for Patricia not to be honest with her, and he loved Toni too much to mess around on her.

Craig turned when he heard the bedroom door open. Patricia walked out stylishly dressed in a short, long-sleeved dress that wrapped across her body and belted on one side, her wavy hair hanging loosely around her shoulders. She sauntered across the room to the mini bar and grabbed a bottle of water.

"Can I offer you something to drink?" she asked, her voice soft and tentative. Craig hated to see her like this, withdrawn and unsure. This was his fault. He knew when he got back involved with her that he wasn't over Toni. He had hoped that spending time with Patricia would make him forget Toni, but that hadn't happened.

"No, I'm good, why don't we have a seat on the sofa." He swept his hand in the direction of the sofa.

"I'd rather stand." Her chin jutted out slightly and she gripped the bottle of water as if it were a lifeline.

Craig walked over and gently took her arm. He guided her to the sofa and they both sat. He wasn't sure where to start. He leaned forward, his elbows on his thighs and his hands clasped together as he stared down at his long tapered fingers.

"There's no sense in me asking if we're breaking up since technically we were never a couple," Patricia spoke softly, sadness fastened on each word.

"I'm sorry, Trish." Craig turned to her. "I hope you know that I truly care about you and that I'll always be here if you need me, but I'm still in love with Toni." He turned away and re-clasped his hands in front of him, twisting the silver and black diamond ring he wore on his left pinky finger.

Silence fell between them and Craig wanted to say more, but had never been good at breaking up with women, though in this case, he and Patricia didn't really have a commitment.

"I guess I should have known this day was coming. Good sex doesn't promise a happily-ever-after," she mumbled and fell back against the sofa. "You could've just called me on the telephone if you didn't want to see me anymore."

"No, I couldn't have." It sickened Craig to know he was hurting her. "Just because we didn't have a commitment doesn't mean I don't care about you."

She fingered the dangling earring hanging from her ear, her gaze on the section of the sofa between them. "Thanks," she said simply, her eyes still lowered.

Craig turned fully in his seat. He lifted her chin with his index finger and forced her to look at him.

"You are a beautiful woman, and I know there is a great guy out there for you. Someone who can love you the way you deserve to be loved. Don't settle, Trish. You deserve to have the happily-ever-after, and I'm sorry I can't give you that."

A small smile tilted the corner of her lip. "Thanks."

Craig sat back on the sofa, glad they were able to talk like adults. Had it been anyone else, he might've wimped out and told her everything over the phone, but he knew Patricia would handle the news with grace and dignity. That's who she was, and he truly hoped that one day she would find her Mr. Right.

"Well since I'm in town, can I at least get dinner or a drink?" She bumped her shoulder against his. "Or does your woman have you on a tight leash and you can't hang out with a friend?"

Craig thought about Toni. *My woman.* "Nah, the least I can do is take you out for something to eat." He stood and helped her up. "What do you have a taste for?"

"Actually, you're in luck. Tonight I'll keep it simple. All I have a taste for is a fat, juicy hamburger and some greasy onion rings."

Craig grinned down at her. "Ahh, a cheap date, my favorite. I actually have the perfect place. Grab what you need and let's go."

**

Toni spun on the bar stool and glanced around the crowded pub. She hadn't been there in months, but couldn't wait to sink her teeth into a double cheeseburger with grilled onions and mushrooms.

Still glancing around the establishment, her gaze connected with a tall, chocolate muscle bound brother who looked as though he spent every waking hour at the gym. He smiled at her, revealing perfectly straight teeth and a dimple in each cheek. *Definitely a cutie.* She nodded and smiled back. A few weeks ago, she would have shot him her come-hither look and allowed him to buy her a drink, but that was before Craig. They'd been back together for almost eight weeks, and their love was growing stronger and stronger each day. Despite her telling Craig that she wanted to take things slowly, she wanted him in every way and right now, no one else would do.

She swung back to the bar just as the bartender asked her cousin for ID. At twenty-three, Jada didn't look a day over eighteen and Toni laughed at the scowl she flashed the bartender.

"I'll have you know that I'm twenty-three," she spat out as she shoved her driver's license at him.

A wolfish grin lit the bartender's face when he glanced at her driver's license. "I'm sorry, sweetheart, but you barely look old enough to drive, let alone drink. I meant no harm. Just doing my job."

Jada straightened her back. Her breasts, barely hidden behind a low cut blouse stood at attention. She flashed her famous smile, the one that no man could resist. "I guess I should be flattered. Hopefully when I'm thirty, you'll still card me."

The bartender's gaze raked across her body and then he leaned in close. "I'm sure I will. Your first drink is on me."

Jada batted her long eyelashes and cupped her hand on top of his. "That's so sweet. Thank you."

Toni rolled her eyes. It wasn't unusual for guys to hit on her and her cousins, but with Jada, it was inevitable. The girl was a walking billboard for anything designer, never going out in public unless her makeup was flawless, her nails were done, and she was dressed to the nines.

"Why are you leading that poor guy on when you know you're not going to give him any play?" Toni whispered.

Jada leaned in close to her. "How else am I going to get my drinks free?"

Toni couldn't help but laugh knowing that her cousin was serious. Jada's life goal was to look good and marry rich. There were only two types of men she dated: Tall, good-looking and wealthy, and tall, good-looking and wealthier than the last. She expected to be wined, dined and presented with expensive gifts. If she thought a guy couldn't meet those qualifications, she had no use for him.

"So where is everyone?" Jada asked, glancing at her diamond platinum watch, a gift from one of her recent boyfriends. "I thought we agreed to meet at seven-thirty, it's almost eight o'clock."

"Well, as usual, Peyton is still at the office trying to do one more thing, but she said she'd be here. MJ called and said she'll be a couple of minutes late. She's finishing up a job, building a porch for somebody."

"I don't know how that girl can leave one job and go to another. Talk about no social life."

Martina and Peyton were two of the hardest working women Toni knew. While Peyton mainly worked the family business, as a carpenter, Martina was always working on projects for someone. Everything from remodeling a basement to building porches and decks, she was never without something to do.

"Everybody can't be like you Jada. Some of us have to work for a living."

Jada turned slightly in her seat. "And what's that supposed to mean? I put in my eight hours. You think it's easy lugging sheet metal around all day? Then I'm dragged down by a tool-belt that weighs a ton and don't even get me started on those steel-toe boots that are murder on my pedicures."

"Oh please, tell it to someone who hasn't seen you in action. I'll admit, you know your stuff when it comes to installing heating and air conditioning units, but you have all the guys who work with behaving like loafer-licking-lackeys. Last time I saw you on a job, some poor kid was carrying your tool belt, following behind you like a lost puppy. So don't—"

"Sorry I'm late you two," Peyton said sliding onto the bar stool next to Toni. "Christina called me just as I was leaving the office. She missed her flight and won't be here until tomorrow morning."

"Hold up," Jada fumed, "you mean to tell me that I turned down a date to be here so that we could celebrate and her butt ain't gon' be here?"

"Yep, so I guess you're stuck with us Your Highness." Peyton called over the bartender. "Where's MJ?"

"Late as usual," Toni answered. "She's on a side job but said she'd be here before eight."

"Did you guys order yet?" Peyton glanced over the menu.

"Why are you studying the menu when you always order the same thing whenever we eat here?"

"Don't start." Peyton rolled her eyes at Toni before directing her attention back to the menu.

"To answer your question," Jada piped in, "we were waiting for the rest of you to show up before we ordered, but considering you guys are always late, or in Christina's case, rarely show up, I don't know why we waited."

Christina or CJ as everyone called her was a journeyman painter and Peyton's little sister. Unlike the rest of their cousins, she was always traveling, sometimes gone for weeks at a time to exotic places like Paris and Thailand. Toni had no idea how she could afford to take so much time off and travel as much as she did on her salary.

"Don't look now, Toni, but your man just walked in," Jada whispered close to her ear.

Toni glanced over her shoulder and smiled at seeing Craig. What were the chances of them ending up at the same bar and grill? "I'll be back," she said to her cousins as she stepped down from the bar stool and pulled the hem of the red one-shoulder blouse down over the top of her black low-rise jeans. Two steps into her walk across the room, she stopped cold. A mounting rage started in her gut and spread through her body. Her fingers balled into a fist, and her nails dug into her palms as she clenched her teeth, unable to keep the bitter taste of fury from spewing out of her mouth. She willed Craig to look her way and within seconds, his eyes met her angry ones.

Toni's gaze landed on the woman glued tightly to his arm and she summoned every ounce of control she could muster not to go over and snatch that hussy by her hair. Toni didn't care if this woman were at least a foot taller than her. All she knew is that her stomach churned with the thought of how amazing Craig's body felt under her touch and knowing another woman was experiencing the same pleasure made her want to spit nails. She didn't know who she was more angry at, him or the wavy-haired vixen at his side.

So it's like that, huh?

She spun on her heels intending to go back to her seat, but a firm grip on her arm stopped her. She glanced up to find the cutie she'd made eye contact with earlier.

"Would you like to dance?" he asked, his voice deep and raspy. His smile was sexy enough to make any woman take a second look.

Toni glanced back at Craig who whispered something to his date and then headed in her direction.

She turned back to Mr. Cutie with the deep voice. "I'd love to dance with you."

***

Craig cursed under his breath when he saw Toni walk away with the guy who looked as if he should be on some football team's offensive line guarding the quarterback.

"Is everything okay?" Patricia asked. "You seem a little tense."

A little tense was putting it mildly. This was one of those moments he wanted to walk over and strangle Toni for overreacting. Didn't she know by now that she was the only woman for him?

"Toni's here and she saw me with you."

Patricia followed his line of vision. "She's cute. I can see why you're infatuated with her. I can go and talk to her if you want."

Craig glanced at Patricia as if she had two heads. He removed his arm from her grasp. "First of all, I'm not infatuated with her I'm in love with her. And secondly, I can speak for myself. I don't need you to say anything to her." The last thing he needed is for her to say anything to Toni.

He spotted Toni on the dance floor. Her hips swirled seductively in front of Muscle Head, not caring that she was making a spectacle of herself. Craig almost popped a vein when the guy wrapped an arm around Toni's waist and pulled her close to the front of his body.

Okay, just calm down, don't make a scene. She's just doing this to get back at me. Craig knew he had to make Toni understand she was the only one for him, despite what the situation looked like, but right now he needed her off that dance floor.

"Hey, I'm sorry," Patricia said, her voice low and contrite. "I didn't mean to sound flippant. I understand what it's like to be in love with someone who might not understand how deep your feelings are."

Craig held her gaze unsure of what to say. Was she saying that she was in love with him? How could that be? As far as he knew, he had never led her to believe that they were anything more than good friends, good friends with benefits.

"Trish, I'm sorry. I shouldn't have snapped. I'm sure this is as awkward for you as it is for me."

"Ya think?" she asked sarcastically. "I hope this all works out between you and Toni." She released his arm.

"You take care of yourself. I'll find my way back to the hotel."

"Wait." Before she walked away, Craig grabbed her wrist. "You came with me, you leave with me. Why don't you get us a table while I try to explain this to Toni. I'll be right back." He didn't wait for a response; instead he glanced at Peyton and Jada and gave a head nod in greeting. Jada grinned, shook her head and turned back to her drink, whereas Peyton threw him a small wave. Craig appreciated them not stepping in, probably because they knew he could handle Toni.

He weaved around tables and sidestepped a few people until he arrived at the dance floor. Not bothering to say anything, he grabbed Toni by the elbow and led her away, shooting her dance partner a lethal glare.

"Craig, get your hands off of me." Toni gritted her teeth. "Who do you think you are man-handling me like this?"

Craig didn't stop until they were outside away from the entrance. "What in the hell is wrong with you?" he said and spun her around.

"Me?" She jabbed her finger into his chest. "You're the one who came up in here with a woman hanging all over you."

"She is just a friend, Toni, and she knows about you."

"And that's supposed to make me feel better?" Toni paced in front of him, her hands on her hips and angry breaths escaping in short spurts. She stopped suddenly. "If she knows about me, I'd assume she knows that we were trying to put our relationship back together. And if that's the case, she should have respected that fact and shouldn't be out with you."

"Come on Toni, you're being unreasonable. She's a friend who happens to be in town. I offered to buy her dinner, and that's it."

Toni threw up her hands. "Well then why are you out here with me? By all means go and buy her dinner."

"Is everything all right out here? You okay, Toni."

Craig turned to find Muscle Head standing a few feet away.

"She's fine." Craig started to turn back to Toni, but realized the guy hadn't budged.

Muscle Head stared Craig down. Craig had to give him credit for not backing down, but he dealt with his kind every day. A guy who pretends to be a good guy to lure some unsuspecting female away and then has his way with her. Oh yeah, Craig knew his type.

"Actually, you can leave 'cause this has nothing to do with you." Craig tried like hell to maintain his cool when what he really wanted to do was slam the guy up against the wall and see if he was packing.

"He was talking to me, Craig, and I can speak for myself!" Though this wasn't a laughing matter, Craig always found it interesting that whenever they argued, her pint-size self would get in his face and talk tough.

"Come on Toni," Muscle Head said, "let's get out of here, maybe grab dinner or catch a movie."

Craig turned fully to face the guy and stepped to him. "You must be crazy if you think I'm letting her go anywhere with you."

"Excuse me!" Toni yanked on Craig's arm, forcing him to face her. "You don't get to say what I'm going to do or not do. You blew that when you walked in there with that … that … woman!"

"I'm not letting you go anywhere with this guy!" Craig roared.

"Stop it you two! You're making a scene," Peyton said and yanked on both their arms. "Toni, come back inside and quit being silly."

Toni ignored Peyton and continued to glare at Craig. "No, I think I'm going to take Anthony up on his offer of dinner and a movie."

"And I said you're not going anywhere with him!" Craig grabbed her upper arm to keep her in place.

Toni jerked back, her eyes stretched wide. Craig couldn't believe he saw fear in her eyes. Did she honestly think he would hurt her? He released her arm and tried to rein in his temper, his heart pumping like a ticking time bomb within his chest. He pulled in a deep breath, his lungs filled with air, and then he released it slowly.

"I know you're mad at me and you have every right to be," he finally said. At that moment, Patricia stepped outside. At first he thought she would approach them, but was grateful when she hung back. "Listen, baby, I don't want you to go anywhere with him. It's not safe. Don't do this just because you're angry at me."

Peyton grabbed hold of the back of Toni's shirt when she started to move away from Craig. "Toni, this is no time to be stubborn. "You don't know this guy. How are you even thinking about going anywhere with him?"

Toni pulled out of Peyton's grasp. "I know all I need to know. Besides, I'm *single* and can date whoever I want." She moved toward Anthony but stopped and turned. "Oh and Peyton tell Jada I have a ride home."

Craig clenched and unclenched his fist, his heartbeat pounded hard against his chest as Toni walked away. He understood she was angry about seeing him with another woman, but he couldn't believe she was going to leave with a stranger.

"Craig, do something!" Peyton pulled on his shirtsleeve. "Arrest her or something! Just don't let her leave with him."

Heat flushed through his body, and he barely maintained his control. "I can't." He bent forward, his hands on his knees and he sucked in several gulps of air before speaking again. "It's not safe for me to go after her. With what I'm feeling right now, there's no telling what I'd do to Muscle Head."

CHAPTER THIRTEEN

Toni sat quietly in the passenger seat of Anthony's beat-up Cadillac as they traveled out of downtown and headed north toward Avondale. She would never be able to forget the anger and disappointment she saw on Craig's face tonight. Granted she was mad at him and wanted to get back at him for being with another woman, but he didn't deserve the way she treated him. If the last couple of months with him proved anything, it was that he loved her. So then, why was she in a car with a man she didn't know, going to a party at God-knows-where?

I'm a stubborn idiot.

"You know what, Anthony?" She glanced sideways at him, trying to keep as much distance between them as possible. "I'm not going to be much fun tonight. Can you just drop me off at my place?"

Toni tensed when he reached over and placed his large muscled hand on her thigh. Alarm bells blared in her head as she thought of all of the things that could happen to her.

"The party will do you good, take your mind off the fight you had with your man."

My man. She had probably ruined everything between her and Craig. She glanced down at the thick hand Anthony had placed on her thigh and realized the decision to leave with him would rank high on the list of the most asinine decisions she'd made to date.

Character is built by the choices we make. Her grandfather's words rattled around in her mind. Though she had tried to use those words to help her stay on a positive course in life, now all they reminded her of was all the stupid choices she'd been making lately.

"I'll tell you what. We go to the party and if at any point you're not having a good time, we can leave and I'll take you home." He lifted an eyebrow and smiled a beautiful smile. "Deal?"

She returned his smile thinking that maybe going to a party, dancing the night away was what she needed. Besides, Anthony seemed harmless enough. "Deal."

Twenty minutes later, Toni stepped out of the car, glad to be on her own two feet and glanced up and down the street. She thought her truck rode horribly, but her clunker was nothing compared to the loud rattling of his car's engine, and the pain radiating through her butt cheeks from hitting every pothole was proof that he needed new shocks.

"Come on, let's go in."

He wrapped one of his meat-hook-hands around her small hand and guided her up the crack-ridden walkway. Part of her wanted to pull away from his sweaty grasp, but the other part of her was scared to death of the neighborhood. She decided to hold on tight.

The cool night air wrapped around Toni, and she shivered thinking the temperature felt more like March than May. She shoved her free hand in her pocket and hunched her shoulders forward as a sense of foreboding snaked up her spine. As they drew closer to the brick home, covered with bars on every window and a cast-iron outer door, fear settled into her bones. If she had the ability to turn time back and start the entire evening again, she would do things very differently.

Oh God, please keep me safe.

She couldn't remember the last time she prayed, but she found herself mumbling every prayer she'd ever learned as a child.

The only thing that made her feel a little more comfortable was the tune of Beyoncé's latest hit pouring out into the streets. *At least there was an actual party going on.*

"We'll go around to the back," Anthony said, guiding her around the house until she put on the brakes and pulled her hand from his grasp.

"You go ahead. I prefer to go through the front." She already didn't feel comfortable being with him, but there was no way in hell she was going to anybody's back yard with some stranger. She left him standing in the middle of the walkway as she trudged up the five concrete stairs. She knocked on the door and hoped someone inside had a cell phone she could use.

Anthony came up behind her just as a tall, scary-looking guy opened the door.

"Ant, man, why you comin' through the front? You know I said er'body have to use the back."

Anthony placed his arm around Toni's shoulder and said, "Look at my girl, dude." He pointed at Toni. "She got too much class to be usin' the back door. So move your ass out the way so we can get our party on."

It had been a long time since Toni had smoked a joint and the smell of weed hit her like a Mack Truck the moment she stepped across the threshold. *I should have known it was this type of party. Stupid. Stupid. Stupid.*

Anthony held her hand and pulled her through the crowded house. They skirted around small groups of people and then a makeshift dance floor. She couldn't tell if people were dancing or having sex considering all the bumping, grinding and moans floating through the air.

She needed to find a phone. When she asked Anthony to use his, he claimed he didn't have one, which she was sure was a lie. There was no way she was staying at this party, especially seeing what she saw when they walked into the semi-dark kitchen.

"Oh, yeah," Anthony sang, his hands waved in the air and he bounced to the groove of the music flowing in from the front room. "This is where the party's at!"

Toni's hand cupped her mouth as disgust rumbled around in her stomach. *Drugs.* Not only were a couple of people passing a joint around, but at the kitchen table, if you could call it a table, a woman snorted a line of cocaine and then another.

"Move out the way," an old man hunched over a walking cane pushed through the pack, "it's my turn."

Just then, a tall, skinny woman clad in a black and blue corset, garter belt and fishnet stockings bound down the stairs, a lipstick stained cigarette dangling from her mouth. "All right, who's next? And don't even bother comin' up here if you ain't got no money. This," she posed, pointy fire-red nails squeezed her breast and then slid down her body and aimed at her crouch, "ain't free."

"I got you, baby." The tall man who had answered the door for Toni and Anthony earlier pulled out a wad of money. "I hope you got some energy, 'cause I plan to go all night long."

Oh hell no! I have to get out of here. Toni's gaze darted around the room seeking a cell phone, and then she realized Anthony had abandoned her. She walked back to the front room and saw a woman curled up in the corner of the sofa talking on a cell phone. Weed, drugs, prostitution - what next? It was time to admit her stupidity and call someone to come and get her.

"Excuse me. Can I use your phone?"

The woman's eyes perused Toni from head to toe and back again. "What I look like, Ma Bell. Go get yo own damn phone." She dismissed Toni and returned to her conversation as if Toni was not still rooted in place less than a foot away.

Next Toni spotted a man bobbing his head, talking on his cell phone near the make-shift dance floor. She approached the guy the way she knew her cousin Jada would have, more swing in her hips, batting her lashes and her chest poked out.

"Hi, may I use your phone?" Toni twirled a lock of her hair.

His gaze raked over her body similar to the way the woman had, but instead of distaste in his eyes, she saw interest. He smiled. "Sure, baby, let me finish giving the directions to this place to my guy, and then it's all yours."

Toni squeezed her thighs together and bounced from one foot to the other while she waited. She'd had a couple of beers before leaving the pub, and of course her bladder chose that moment to rebel.

"I'll be right back," Toni told the cell phone guy and then went in search of a bathroom.

Upstairs in the bathroom, Toni took care of her business, hurrying to make sure the man with the cell phone didn't disappear. She flushed the toilet and quickly washed her hands, not surprised that there wasn't anything to dry them on. She swiped her hands up and down her jean-clad pant leg and did a quick check of herself in the cracked mirror. Screams and the sound of furniture being tossed around interrupted her calm.

"What the heck is going on down there?"

She turned from the sink and the door to the bathroom burst open. "Police! Hands in the air! Now!"

Toni stood frozen to the creaky floorboards as she stared up at the barrel of a gun aimed at her. A shiver of panic lodged in her chest and fear like she'd never known before gripped her brain.

"I said hands in the air!" The female cop's voice raised an octave.

Toni's body trembled, and she lifted jittery hands. "Wha ... what's going on? I ... I did ... didn't do anything."

"You have the right to remain silent ..."

Tears welled in her eyes. The brutish female police officer slammed her flat against the peeling wallpaper and patted her body down. Toni cried out when her arms were jerked behind her back and cuffs slapped on. *What's going on?* Tears spilled down her cheeks. Did Craig have anything to do with this? Was he trying to scare her by having some of his cop friends hunt her down and then arrest her? If so, his scare tactic worked, but how could he be that cruel? She knew he was angry, but this was going overboard.

"I didn't do anything," Toni cried. The officer grabbed her cuffed wrists and shoved her out of the bathroom. "If Craig sent you to scare me, it worked. Please, just take the cuffs off. They're too tight and they're cutting off my circulation."

The officer escorted her through the second level of the house, and Toni couldn't believe her eyes. Cops everywhere. They herded partygoers out of the house and into police vans, and realization dawned on her. *This has nothing to do with Craig.* Fear settled into her bones. Bright lights flashed in her eyes as she stumbled toward the waiting police van. *Oh my God, the media is here.*

She didn't know what was happening, but she'd never felt as alone and afraid as she did at that moment.

***

Craig paced the length of the family room his anger mounted with each step. *Where in the hell is she?* After taking Patricia back to her hotel, he had driven by Toni's house only to find it dark and no Toni. He then called to see if Peyton or Jada had talked with her. Neither had seen or heard from her. He didn't know what he would do if anything happened to her. He responded to hundreds of domestic violence calls a year and knew that all it took was for one guy, to think she was a tease, and things could go horribly wrong for her.

He growled and swiped his arm across the fireplace mantle. Frustration engulfed his body as he watched an expensive vase and framed photos hit a nearby wall, shards of glass scattered across his carpeted floor.

"Where are you, dammit?"

He didn't know what else to do. He'd driven to a few of her favorite spots, hoping to find her, preferably alone, but most importantly safe. He thought about calling in a favor and having her located via her cell phone, but Peyton had her purse with her, meaning if Toni were in trouble, she wouldn't be able to contact anyone.

He glanced at his watch again, at least the thirtieth time in the past hour, only to find that it was two minutes past the last time he checked. *Two-fifteen in the morning.* Peyton had called him an hour ago asking if he'd heard from Toni yet. She and Jada had gone to Toni's house after leaving the pub and found out what he'd already found out. Toni wasn't home.

The sound of his cell phone pierced through the quietness of the room and Craig practically slid across the table to answer it.

Glancing at the screen, he recognized the number. "Yeah, this is Logan."

"Craig man, you might want to get down to the station," Paul, a fellow cop, said. "Your ex, Toni, was arrested a few hours ago, in a drug raid. She was cleared of all charges, but she's still here. I think ..."

Craig snatched his keys from the entryway table and headed to the garage, barely hearing anything else Paul said. All he knew was that he needed to get to her.

Fifteen minutes later, Craig rushed through the door of the police station acknowledging a few cops but focusing on finding Toni. He spotted Paul, who nodded his head toward the lone body sitting in a hardwood chair, her head rested against the wall. Craig studied Toni from a distance, and her eyes didn't blink as she stared straight ahead.

His gaze traveled over her, and though she appeared to be fine, something was definitely wrong. He slowly moved across the room, not taking his eyes off her. He claimed the seat to her left and sat without speaking. All he wanted was to pull her into his arms and hold her, but instead he sat in silence.

"I didn't call you," she said, her whisper choked by tears. She turned to him and a tear slid down her cheek. First one, and then more followed. "Why are you here?"

"Oh, baby," he said, his heart breaking at the anguish he saw on her face. "I'm here to take you home."

She fell into his welcoming arms, her loud sobs smothered by his chest and Craig didn't think he would ever let her go. Relief like he'd never known before flooded his body as he kissed the top of her head and rocked her body. Tonight he'd experienced what she probably experienced whenever he left for work. A helpless fear of not knowing if the person you loved, were safe.

Craig held her for what seemed like forever until her tears subsided.

"You shouldn't be nice to me," she said against his now damp shirt. He handed her a tissue from a nearby Kleenex box. She lifted her head, tears hanging on her long eyelashes. "I don't deserve you."

"Don't say that. Don't ever say that." He pulled her back to him and kissed the top of her head again. "Come on, let's get out of here."

Craig walked with her, holding her close to his body. When she stumbled a second time, he lifted her into his arms and proceeded out of the station. It wasn't enough to have her wrapped in his arms. He wanted to take her home and never let her out of his sight again. He also wanted to know everything that happened tonight, but he wouldn't push. He'd let her tell him in her own time and if she didn't, he could always read the report.

Silence filled the car until she realized he was heading to her house.

"I don't want to go home," she stole a glance at him and then dropped her gaze.

Craig slowed the car. "Where do you want me to take you? To Peyton's? Your parents? Your grandparents? I'll take you wherever you want to go."

She covered her face with her hands and her shoulders shook violently as her sobs filled the car's interior. Craig had never felt so helpless in all of his life. Checking his mirrors, he pulled over to the side of the road, fearing that something else happened tonight.

"Toni, talk to me." He gathered her in his arms as close as the center console would allow and held her. "Baby, I know I said I'll always have a shoulder for you to cry on, but you're killing me here. What can I do? Tell me what you need from me. Anything."

She lifted her head, tears streaming down her face. "I can't go home."

Craig stiffened. Unease crawled up his spine and the worse possible scenarios of what happened tonight filled his mind. "Why not? What happened? Did someone hurt you?" His tone rougher than he intended. "Because if someone laid a hand on you I will—"

"No. No, nothing happened." She shook her head and held onto his arm. "No one did anything to me. I just can't go home. I don't want to be alone. I can't go to any of my family because I can't bear to see the disappointment in their eyes."

Craig released the breath he didn't realize he was holding. "Honey, they love you. Even if they are disappointed, they're more worried than anything."

"I know, but I can't face them right now."

He wiped her tears with the pad of his thumb then replaced his finger with his lips, kissing her cheeks. "All right, just stop crying. Everything is going to be fine."

He released her and steered back into traffic. Making a u-turn, he headed for his house and dialed Peyton.

***

Toni followed Craig upstairs and was surprised when he turned left toward the guest room instead of heading to his bedroom. She didn't want to be alone. Even if he were only a few doors away, it would be still too far. She wanted to be in his arms, but she didn't have the right. Thinking about the way she'd treated him hours ago made her sick. She knew the type of man he was: honorable, dependable and loyal. When he told her the woman he was with earlier was just a friend, she knew he was telling the truth, but at the time, she wanted to hurt him.

"The bathroom should have everything you need." He flicked the light on. "I'll be right back. I'm going to find something for you to sleep in."

How could she tell him she wanted to be with him tonight, that she needed to be with him tonight? It was past time for her to talk to him, to be honest about their breakup and her behavior over the past few months.

Craig walked back into the room, and she hadn't moved from the spot near the door.

"Here's a T-shirt and some socks. I know how much you hate walking around barefoot." His voice was as gentle as the love shimmering in his eyes.

Toni almost cried all over again at his thoughtfulness. She accepted the socks, but only stared at the shirt that he held in his other hand.

Craig glanced down at the T-shirt and then back at her. "It's okay, it's clean."

She swallowed and tears popped into her eyes. "I don't want that one," she said just above a whisper.

Craig dropped his hand to his side and lifted an eyebrow. "Excuse me?"

"I want the burgundy one." She stared into his confused eyes. "The one that says 'I do my best work undercover'. The one I use to sleep in when … after you were shot and when you worked late."

They stared at each other for the longest, but then Craig dropped the shirt on the floor and roughly pulled her into his arms.

"You scared me to death tonight." He squeezed her tighter, and she could have sworn that she heard him sniff. Was he crying? "*If you ever* do anything like what you did tonight, I will lock you up myself."

"Craig," she said gasping for air, "I can't breathe."

He loosened his hold but didn't let go. Wrapping her arms around his narrow waist, she laid her head against his chest and listened to the erratic beat of his heart.

"I am so sorry for everything. I'll never be able to apologize enough for my behavior tonight." She lifted her head and met his gaze, not missing the redness in his eyes. Tonight she had fed into all that he feared most – a woman hurt by the hands of a man. "I promise I will never put you or myself through what I put us through tonight."

He pushed the hair from her face and covered her mouth. His tongue slipped between her lips, caressing, teasing, devouring. The love she had for him intensified with every stroke of his tongue, and she knew there was no other place she'd rather be than right there in his arms.

Toni groaned when Craig ended the kiss way too soon. He grabbed her hand and led her to the bed.

"I need you to tell me what's going on with you, and I want the truth. I don't care what it is. I need you to talk to me." He stared down at their joined fingers. His thumb caressed the back of her hand. "I know you've been keeping something from me, and I'm pretty sure it has to do with why you ended our relationship." He looked up at her. "I need you to trust me. Tell me what is standing between you, me and our future."

It was now or never. Toni had to tell him. If she didn't, she knew she'd lose him for good. On the other hand, if she did tell him, what would he think of her?

"Toni, I love you more than I thought I could ever love another human being, but if we don't have honesty and trust, we can't move forward." He lifted their joined hands to his lips and kissed the back of hers.

She sighed and met his gaze. "I had an abortion."

CHAPTER FOURTEEN

For a moment, Craig sat stunned, finding it hard to believe the words that came from her mouth, but suddenly heat flushed through his body, and a mounting rage propelled him off the bed. He stumbled back and put as much distance between them as the space would allow.

Anger strangled him as he stared at her. "You were pregnant?" he managed to ask. Bracing himself against the wall his breaths were labored as if a two-ton boulder sat on his chest. She knew how much he wanted a family, and she had the nerve to stand before him and tell him that she had an abortion. "You killed my child ... *our* child?" He couldn't believe this was happening.

Toni's mouth fell open, and her eyes bulged. She leaped from the bed. "No! No, you don't understand," she stammered. "Let me explain."

"No!" He jerked his arm out of her grasp and moved across the room, his legs barely able to support his weight. "It's you who don't fucking understand!" he roared, and she staggered back. "You had a damn abortion knowing how much I wanted a family. How much I wanted you and me to get married, and have children. And you're telling me something like this?"

"Craig, please listen to me!"

He teetered on the edge of reality and fog clouded the part of his brain that refused to listen to anything else she had to say. Instead, the words *I had an abortion* taunted him.

He bumped into the wall, his back resting against the cool surface. His hands gripped the side of his head trying to stop the room from spinning. He hadn't felt this type of pain, this type of hurt since he found out Cynthia had been killed.

He startled when she threw a large glass vase, so close to his head that he felt the vibrations, bounce off the wall. He quickly turned to Toni, noticing for the first time the wild look in her eyes.

"I said listen to me, dammit! When I was *raped*," she screamed, her face contorted and her eyes blazed with hurt and defeat. "I got pregnant and that was when I had the abortion. I would never, *ever* abort your child, *our* child. How could you even think I would ever do something like that?"

Her loud sobs filled the room and Craig finally understood. *I would never, ever abort your child, our child.* He played the words back again in his head. *I would never, ever abort your child, our child.*

The fog in his brain cleared, and everything became clear.

Oh dear God. He crossed the room in two long steps and pulled her roughly against his chest. "I am so sorry. Oh my God, baby, I am so sorry." This time he didn't bother holding his emotion back as tears filled his eyes.

What had he done? She bared her soul to him and he had turned his back on her. Just that quick. After telling her that they could get through anything, that he'd always be there for her.

"Baby, please forgive me. I am so sorry I didn't listen to you." He held her face in his hand, forcing her to look at him. "I … I …"

"Shh," she said through her tears and wrapped her arms tightly around his neck. "I'm the one who is sorry."

***

Hours later, Toni lay in the crook of Craig's arms feeling as if she'd been dragged through a landmine. Too exhausted to make the short walk to the bed, they fell asleep in each other's arms right there on the floor.

The events of the night before weighed heavy on Toni and she didn't know if Craig would be able to forgive her, or if she could forgive herself. Arguing with him at the pub and then leaving with Anthony was one of the most dangerous decisions she'd ever made and wouldn't soon forget. If anyone were to ask her why she reacted the way she did, she didn't think she could give them an answer that made any sense. She had selfishly put them through an emotional hell all because she was too stubborn and too quick to cop an attitude, instead of remembering all the reasons she had fallen in love with Craig.

"What are you thinking about?"

Surprised, Toni's gaze shot up and she met Craig's tired, red eyes.

"You," she said her hands rubbing lightly against his chest. "I was thinking about you."

"What about me?" He ran his hand through her hair, pushing strands away from her face and then allowing his hand to linger near her temple.

She hesitated, but then said. "I don't think I can live without you."

A small smile lifted the right side of his mouth. "That's good because I know I can't live without you."

Toni held his gaze for a few seconds before lifting up. Her back protested at the sudden move, and a groan slipped through her lips. She couldn't remember the last time she'd slept on the floor.

"You okay?" Craig sat up quick, his hand rubbing her back. "I guess the floor wasn't a good idea, huh?"

She shook her head. They both slid back and propped up against the wall. They sat in silence until Toni said, "I'm ready to tell you everything."

"In that case, let's take this conversation to the bed." They climbed on the bed fully dressed in the clothes they had on the night before. "Before you tell me anything, I have to make sure you forgive me for jumping to conclusions last night. I could blame my lack of understanding on the hellish night I had, emotional exhaustion or whatever, but I'll never be able to apologize to you enough for my reaction. The things I said to you last night, or for the way I treated you."

"Craig, honey, I don't blame you for the misunderstanding last night. I think you reacted the way any man would react if the woman he was sleeping with suddenly informed him she had an abortion." She took a deep breath and released it slowly. "I have wanted to tell you about the abortion since the first time you asked me to marry you, but I could never drum up the courage.

Ending that pregnancy was the hardest thing I've ever had to do in my life."

"Why were you afraid to tell me?"

"Because ..." she glanced down at their joined hands and readjusted her head against his chest, "It was bad enough deciding to have the abortion, but it was worse that I had the procedure done at an underground place. The facility wasn't the most sanitized, and I'm not even sure they knew what they were doing. All I know is that, though I'm not pro-abortions, I couldn't have a child that was a result of a rape and I'll live with that guilt until the day I die." She closed her eyes for a moment to prepare for what she had to tell him next. "There's a lot of scarring, I can't have children."

Seconds passed without either of them speaking until Craig said, "For years, I've talked about one day getting married and having children." He lifted her chin, forcing her to look at him. "But I've waited a lifetime for you. Whether we have children someday or not, as long as I have you, I have everything I need." He kissed her lips. "I am sorry you didn't feel you could tell me and that this secret has kept us apart for so long. Baby, I love you, whether we have children or not - *I love you*."

***

Craig stood in the bedroom doorway and watched Toni as she dressed. She knew she would hear from her grandfather, especially since the drug raid made the news, but Craig wasn't sure how she would feel about being called into a meeting at her grandparent's house this morning.

"Hey," she said when she looked up. She slid her belt through the belt-loops of her jeans. "Why are you just standing there? Is everything okay?"

He walked farther into the room and reached for her hand, bringing it to his lips and then pulling her close. "Everything's fine, but Peyton called."

Toni stiffened in his arms. "What did she say?"

"She said your grandfather wants to see you. He wants you to be at their house at eleven."

She glanced at the time, and the digital clock read nine forty-five. She groaned and slumped against Craig. "Well, I guess I'd better get ready to go. Would you mind dropping me off at home so I can pick up my truck and change clothes?"

"I don't mind at all, but I was thinking that maybe I'll go with you if that's okay."

"You would do that?" She removed small bits of lint from his T-shirt, not meeting his gaze.

He pulled gently down on the ponytail at the back of her head, forcing their eyes to meet. "Of course. I'd do anything for you."

***

Being summoned to a meeting with her grandfather was like being summoned to court. You might expect things to go one way, but chances were there would be some surprises. Toni had no doubt this meeting would be the same.

"Are you all right?" Craig asked and squeezed her hand. "You look like you're going to be sick."

"I feel like I'm going to be sick," she mumbled when Craig pulled up to her grandparent's estate and she noticed all the cars in the driveway. "I thought I was just meeting with Grampa. This looks like a family meeting." Apprehension bounced around in her gut, and her stomach muscles tightened as she thought about what her family would say regarding her recent behavior.

She and Craig entered through the back door and made their way toward the front of the house. Her heels clicking against the marble floor did nothing to drown out the sound of her pulse pounding in her ears. Nor did the smell of food or the bouts of laughter she heard ease the tension crawling up her back.

Just breathe. She told herself over and over again until Craig tugged on her hand, halting her steps.

"Why are you so nervous?" he asked when he put his arm around her shoulder and pulled her part way down another hall that led to her grandfather's study. "Your family loves you almost as much as I do. As for your grandfather, I'm sure he's just going to tell you how disappointed he is, but that he still loves you."

Her grandfather was always quick to tell them how much he loved them and how proud he was of each of them. It was the thought of disappointing him that broke Toni's heart.

"I'll be right here waiting for you."

Toni tensed. "What? You're not coming with me?" she whispered, panic rioting within her. She assumed that when he agreed to come with her that he intended to sit in on the meeting. "As far as I'm concerned, you're family and I know I'm not the only one who feels that way." She reached for his hand and drummed up some courage before they headed toward all of the conversation coming from the room.

Toni's steps faltered when she reached the family room's opening. She knew by the number of cars outside that many of her family members were present, but as she glanced around at the suddenly silent group, it appeared the whole Jenkins clan were in attendance even Christina.

"Ah, well if it isn't our TV star daughter," her father cracked and walked over to shake Craig's hand. "Good to see you again, Craig."

"You too, Mr. Jenkins."

"What is this, an intervention or something?" Toni asked, anger twisted in her gut. "Because if it is, I'm not interested. I know I messed up and I'm sorry. I don't need any of you telling me how stupid I am or how my character is built by my decisions or that my de … decisions are …" Her arms flailed around while she tried to keep her tears at bay. "I don't need an intervention," she said on a sob.

She felt the warmth of Craig's hand against her back, as if he were saying to calm down.

"Call it what you want, young lady, but your behavior is clearly out of control when you get caught on television leaving a drug house." Her father ran his hand through his full head of dark hair and walked back over to stand near Toni's mother.

"It wasn't a drug house," Toni said quietly, knowing that none of them wanted to hear her excuses or explanations.

"Honey." Her mother walked across the room and stopped in front of her. Toni stiffened when her mother reached for her hand. Natalie Jenkins rarely showed compassion and Toni didn't know what to make of her mother holding her hand. "We're not trying to do an intervention, but I think something needs to be said. You're a beautiful, intelligent woman, you don't need to be dating drunks or hanging out at drug houses. Someone might mistake you for a slut or something. We didn't raise you to be a whore and—"

"Okay, that's enough!" Steven Jenkins's voice boomed from his spot near the fireplace.

Katherine Jenkins hurried over and pulled her granddaughter in for a quick hug. "Everything is going to be just fine, sweetheart." She kissed her on the cheek and then released Toni, and turned to hug Craig.

Steven Jenkins moved toward Toni and she studied his face. She didn't see disappointment, or anger. What she saw was the man who loved and adored her.

"Hi sweetheart," he said and pulled her into his arms.

Tears she could no longer hold back spilled from her eyes and her body shook with sobs that rocked her to the core. She could sense Craig nearby, but her grandfather didn't release her instead he said to Craig, "She's all right, son. She'll be all right."

Toni threw her arms around her grandfather's midsection and held on tight. The familiar woodsy scent of his cologne that he'd worn for as long as she could remember calmed her the way a pacifier soothed a baby. She couldn't imagine her life without the man who had always come to her defense and never judged her.

Toni didn't know how long they stood there, but she didn't want to let go when her grandfather placed a kiss on her forehead and stepped back. She ran her hands down her face and took a deep breath. She'd done more crying in the last couple of days than she had all year and hoped her life would get back on track soon.

Her grandfather moved to the side. Aunts, uncles and cousins all greeted her, telling her not to worry and that everything was going to be fine. Toni always felt that her family was her rock, and their display of love right now made her realize just how important they were in her life.

"You two come in and have a seat," her grandfather said motioning her and Craig to the sofa. "How are you young man? It's good to see you again," Steven said to Craig and patted him on the shoulder.

"You too, Sir," Craig said absently, his focus solely on Toni as he opened his arms to her.

"You okay?" he asked for what seemed like the hundredth time since he picked her up from the police station the night before.

Toni nodded and wiped her face with the back of her hand. She was an emotional wreck and couldn't wait for this all to be over. Craig led them to the extra long sofa where Peyton, Jada and Kevin were sitting.

"Hey," Peyton said when Toni and Craig sat next to her. Peyton gave her a one-arm hug. "I'm glad you're okay," she whispered and handed Toni the handbag that she'd left at the pub.

"Thanks." Toni, surprised she still had tears left, wiped them away as fast as they fell. "I'm so sorry for the way I acted last night. I was way out of line."

Peyton squeezed her free hand. "Don't worry."

Steven Jenkins lounged in his favorite recliner and sipped from a glass of cranberry juice before he spoke. "I called everyone here today not necessarily to discuss what happened last night with Toni, but to give you all a few reminders. Katherine and I have worked too hard to build a legacy for this family to have any of you come along and destroy it with one bad decision. You all need to remember that when you're out there in public, it's not just you people see. You represent the Jenkins family. The things you do and the choices you make don't only affect you, they affect all of us."

Toni stared down at her hands embarrassed by her behavior the night before and even more so now that everyone had been summoned to an impromptu family meeting.

"Toni, I'm not sure if you know this," her grandfather continued, "but we have been inundated with calls from the media since early this morning, asking us why you were hanging out at a drug house and whether or not we knew you were on drugs. And my personal favorite: are there other members of the Jenkins' family battling drug addictions."

"Grampa," Toni started but stopped when he raised his forefinger.

"I'm not going to give you a long drawn out speech, sweetheart. I know you regret all that happened last night. No matter what the media says, we are the Jenkins. We stick together and support each other."

"Come on dad." Toni's father leaped from his seat. "You have to stop coddling her! That's why she carries on the way she does. You've babied her since the day she was born, and it has to stop!"

Her grandfather rose to his full height of six-foot-one and glared at his son. "Who do you think you're talking to?" He stood within a foot of Joseph. "I don't care how old you are, you *will* respect me in my house!"

Joseph held his hands out. "I'm sorry dad. I meant no disrespect. It's just that this is so typical Toni and you're making it seem like her behavior is acceptable, when it's not."

"Joseph," Steven leaned against the back of his recliner and glared at his son. "Have you forgotten all the crap you pulled when you were younger?" His siblings laughed and began talking amongst themselves until

Steven hushed everyone. "And if I remember correctly you too had a couple of trips to the police station. So I don't understand why you're being so critical of her mistakes."

Silence settled over the room and Toni wondered why she'd never heard any stories about her father getting into trouble.

"I'm harder on her because she's a female," Toni's father explained. "She is out here with all of these idiots who don't give a damn that she's a wonderful young lady trying to find her place in this crazy world or that she's a Jenkins. Anything could have happened to her at that house last night, and I wouldn't have known. I wouldn't have been able to protect my child," her father choked out, his voice loaded with emotion. He moved across the room and pulled Toni into his arms, holding her tight. When Natalie came over, he pulled her into their small group hug. A few moments passed before they released Toni and headed for the door hand in hand.

Toni stood stunned. In all her twenty-nine years she couldn't remember her father ever saying anything that would make her think he cared about her well-being. And a hug from both her parents, at the same time, totally threw her off balance.

Steven Jenkins didn't speak for a few minutes, but then said, "Can everyone excuse us for a minute? I'd like to talk to my granddaughter alone."

Craig didn't budge and Toni loved him even more if that were possible. It wasn't until her grandfather put his hand on Craig's shoulder and said, "I only want to talk to her. She'll be okay with me."

Toni squeezed Craig's hand and tried to smile to reassure him that he could go, but deep down inside, she didn't want him to leave, ever.

"Come on dear," Toni's grandmother said to Craig and gently pulled on his arm, forcing him to stand. "Come and hang out with an old lady, have something to eat and tell me why we don't see you more often."

"I'll be right down the hall if you need me," Craig said over his shoulder as Toni's grandmother ushered him out of the room.

She nodded and watched everyone pile out of the room, including her Grandfather who promised he'd be right back. Toni glanced around and recalled the number of times she and her cousins hung out in the huge room, playing hide-go-seek or tag. She almost laughed when she thought about the time Martina had dared Christina to climb the wall-to-wall bookcase. She had never seen her grandfather as mad as he was when he walked in and found Christina underneath a mound of books crying.

Steven Jenkins walked back into the room with a bottle of cranberry-orange juice and handed it to Toni. She smiled thinking about how he usually started his "talks" to her with a bottle of her favorite juice.

"So do you want to tell me what's been going on these past few months? I've noticed a change in you, but had hoped that whatever was bothering you would be fixed by now."

Toni shook her head. She didn't know where to start since she wasn't sure herself. All she knew is that after she had broken up with Craig, she lost a part of herself. She didn't want to think, and she didn't want to feel, and that's what she told her grandfather.

He pushed back on the sofa and crossed one of his ankles over his knee. "Sweetheart, there's something you should remember."

She sat back on the sofa and took a swig from her juice. "And what's that?"

"That whatever you put out there in the universe is what you're going to get back." He patted her hand that rested on the sofa cushion between them. "If you allow negativity to be a part of your life, that's what you're going to attract. The same thing goes for confusion. To use your cousin Jada's words – if you don't have your shit together then you—"

Toni fell out laughing. She was sure her cousin hadn't cursed around their grandfather, but the idea of him quoting her cousin was scarier than her time spent at the police station.

"I think I get it, Grampa." Toni dabbed at her eyes still laughing. "I'll make sure I get my uh, stuff together."

Her grandfather wrapped his long arm around her shoulder. "I know sweetheart. Now getting back to what happened last night. I know you're not on drugs or involved in some type of prostitution ring like the media's claiming, and I also know – that you know - how I feel about negative press."

Toni felt pieces of her heart cracking like glass into tiny slivers within the confines of her chest. Her family was her world, and one stupid decision could have caused their world to fall apart, and it would be her fault.

"As I said earlier, you know as well as I do," her grandfather continued, "that the choices you make don't only affect you, they affect all of us in some way. After you and I finish here, Peyton and I have work to do. We have to make sure that our clients know that Jenkins &

Sons Construction is as solid as it has always been. We don't want them to buy into what the media is spewing - that our trades people and technicians are on drugs. We have to make sure that drama like what happened last night won't be brought into their homes and businesses by us. So the next time you want to rebel, remember that you're a reflection of me and you're a reflection of this family."

"I know, Grampa. Whatever you need me to do to make this right I will, and I promise nothing like this will ever happen again."

He kissed her on the cheek. "Okay, on to another subject. By the looks of things, I'd say you and your young man are working things out."

Toni placed her hand against her chest, humbled that she and Craig were going to work on their relationship.

"Craig is amazing. We're going to give our relationship another try."

"Good, I think he's perfect for you. He's a nice young man and he's a cop. So if something like what happened last night happens again, he can probably get you out of jail fairly quick."

Toni laughed. "Oh, Grampa. I love you so much."

"I love you too, sweetheart and I always will."

"Are you two done?" Her grandmother stood in the doorway. "There's a handsome man out here who is anxious to see my granddaughter."

"You mean our granddaughter."

"Yeah, whatever." Her grandmother waved him off and Craig stepped into the room, followed by her parents.

"Honey, we're sorry about our attitude earlier," her mother said and hugged her.

"Yeah, we don't want you to think that we don't love you, because we do. We love you very much," her father said and pulled her into his arms for a hug.

Two hugs in one day. Toni didn't want to let go, not until her gaze met Craig's, where he stood just inside the door. Her father released her and told her that there was food in the kitchen if she was hungry, but she barely acknowledged his comment. Instead, she couldn't take her eyes off the man she loved. The man she wanted to spend the rest of her life with.

"Are you okay?" Craig asked when everyone left them alone.

"I'm fine and if you ask me that again, I'm going to scream."

"Is that right?" He pulled her into his arms and made slow work of kissing her. "How about if I tell you that I love you?" He mumbled against her mouth.

"What was that? I didn't understand you."

He lifted his head and grinned. "I *said* I love you."

She cupped his cheek with her hand. "And I love you too and I always will."

Two Months Later

Craig trudged into the house after working a double, barely able to stand on his two feet. He didn't know how much more he could take. The long hours were taking a toll on his body and leaving the police force was starting to sound better and better each day. He dropped his bag near the door that he'd just entered and placed his keys on top of the refrigerator. Maybe his brother Derek was right. Maybe it was time to pursue another career using his Criminal Justice degree. The only problem – would he be able to let go of his obsession to rid the city of jerks like Thomas James?

The thought of Thomas brought a slight pep into Craig's step when he sauntered over to the stove. They'd found and arrested the low-down dirty dog earlier that evening and the knowledge that Thomas faced charges that could keep him in prison for life was the highlight of Craig's evening.

"Mmm, something smells good," Craig mumbled and lifted the lids of the pots that were on the stove. His mouth watered at the sight - steak and onions, broccoli and his all time favorite, mashed potatoes. Toni was spoiling him. Lately, he arrived home to a home cooked meal, something that he was quickly getting used to.

It had been two months since the night of her arrest and their relationship was getting stronger by the day, promising a happily-ever-after. He patted his front pants pocket to make sure he had the small velvet box that held the two-carat emerald cut diamond that he'd carried around for months. Tonight he planned to ask her to be his wife.

He replaced the lids on the pots, suddenly not as hungry and tired as he was when he first walked in. He took the stairs two at a time in search of his future wife.

"Toni?" he called out when he reached the upstairs landing. "I'm home!"

He walked into his bedroom and noticed the bedding was turned down, but no Toni. The bathroom door was closed and he assumed she was in there. A grin spread across his face. Maybe she was planning one of her surprises. The one where she steps out in sexy lingerie and showed him how much she'd missed him.

He hurried, kicked off his shoes, and snatched his shirt off tossing it in a nearby chair. It was then he realized she hadn't responded when he called out.

"Toni?" he called again and moved closer to the bathroom door. Concern niggled at his peace of mind. "Baby, you in there?"

He put his ear to the door and that's when he heard her. Crying.

Not bothering to knock again he turned the knob, glad the door wasn't locked but prepared to knock it down if he had to. He walked in to find Toni sitting on the edge of the Jacuzzi tub, tears streaming down her face.

Craig could handle difficult criminals, but Toni crying, he still couldn't deal with.

"Hey, what's going on?" He stood near the vanity and did a quick once over. Not seeing anything physically wrong, he took note of her wearing his T-shirt and nothing else. He squatted down on his haunches in front of her. "Did something happen?" he asked then chided himself for asking a stupid question knowing that she wouldn't be crying for no reason.

"Yes," she sobbed and lunged at him, knocking the breath out of him. He held them both steady with one hand braced on the floor behind him and the other around her midsection. Her arms clasped tightly around his neck like a vise squeezing a slice of bread.

Eventually, Craig caught his breath. He snaked both arms around her narrow waist and stood with her securely against him, her legs automatically wrapped around him. Everything about this woman, *his woman*, made him want to protect her and keep her happy.

He carried Toni out of the bathroom and didn't stop walking until they reached the bed where he set her down. He sat next to her and for the first time noticed the white stick in her hand.

"What happened?" He kissed her and rubbed her back for a few moments, hoping she'd tell him what was wrong. "Why were you crying?"

She handed him the white stick. "I'm ... I'm pregnant."

Craig held the stick between his thumb and index finger. He didn't know how long he sat there processing her words while the plus sign on the stick stood out like a big, blinking neon sign.

"What? How is that ..." he stopped. The rest of his words lodged in his throat as his pulse thumped wildly. He glanced at her and just above a whisper asked, "Are you sure?"

She nodded. "I'm pretty sure. I'm three weeks late, and it's positive." She pointed at the stick. "I'll call tomorrow for a doctor's appointment so that we can be absolutely sure, but I'm pretty sure."

Craig sat stunned for a few minutes longer and then leaped off the bed and into the air. "Woo hoo! Yeah, baby!" he yelled punching his fist in the air. He turned to her and blinked back unexpected tears that he refuse to let fall. Then scooped her off the bed and into his arms, her feet dangling off the floor. "You've made me the happiest man alive. I can't believe it. We're having a baby!"

His mouth covered hers and he kissed her softly. He needed Toni to feel how much he loved her. Needed her to know he could never live without her. And then he had to know. He suddenly released her lips.

"The tears from earlier," he said, pleading in his voice, "please tell me those were tears of joy and that you're happy about this."

"I'm ... I'm shocked," she said, her hands gripping his shoulders, her lips moist from their kiss as she stared into his eyes. "But I am more than happy. The thought of having your baby, our baby, is like a dream come true. No, no it's more than a dream come true."

He pulled her against his body and held her tight. "Thank you," he said hoarsely into her hair. "Having you *and* our baby means everything to me."

"I still can't believe I'm pregnant," she said when he set her on her feet. She paced in front of the bed. "I can't believe it," she repeated more to herself than to him as her hand moved in circles lovingly over her flat stomach.

Craig grabbed Toni's hand to stop her from pacing. She met his gaze and then spotted the black velvet box that he'd pulled from his pocket.

"The timing of your news is perfect because tonight I wanted to ask you something." He bent down on one knee and didn't miss the new set of tears filling her eyes.

"Oh my God," she whispered, her hands shaking against her lips.

"Toni TJ Jenkins, you are a godsend. When we first met, you pretty much cursed me out for not taking you and your career seriously, calling me all types of asshole. I never would have guessed that I would fall hopelessly in love with you, a plumber." He grinned when her brows drew together and her hands flew to her hips. He quickly continued. "I love everything about you from your melodious laugh, your quick wit, to that stubborn streak that runs deep. Baby, you're everything I've always wanted in a wife and everything I didn't know I needed in my life. I love you more than I'll ever be able to express. Would you do me the honor of becoming my wife? Will you marry me?"

She squealed and jumped up and down a few times before stopping to place her hands on each side of his face, her beautiful lips inches from his. "Yes, yes, yes! I love you so much. I'd be honored to be your wife!"

The End

If you enjoyed this book by Sharon C. Cooper,
please consider leaving a review on any online book site,
review site or social media outlet!

ABOUT THE AUTHOR

Bestselling author, Sharon C. Cooper, hasn't always been tied to a desk, a computer and a chair. Earlier in life, Sharon spent 10 years as a sheet metal worker. And while enjoying that unique line of work, she obtained her B.A. in Business Management with an emphasis in Communication.

Sharon is a romance-a-holic - loving anything that involves romance with a happily-ever-after, whether in books, movies or real life. She writes contemporary romance, as well as romantic suspense and enjoys rainy days, carpet picnics, and peanut butter and jelly sandwiches. When Sharon is not writing or working, she's hanging out with her amazing husband, doing volunteer work or reading a good book (a romance of course). To read more about Sharon and her novels, visit www.SharonCooper.net.

OTHER TITLES BY SHARON C. COOPER

Something New ("Edgy" Sweet Romance)

Best Woman for the Job
(Short Story - Contemporary Romance)

Blue Roses (Romantic Suspense)

Secret Rendezvous
(Prequel to Rendezvous with Danger - Romantic Suspense)

Rendezvous with Danger (Romantic Suspense)

***

January – 2014 – *Truth or Consequences*
Reunited Series (book 3)

April - 2014 – *All You'll Ever Need*
The Jenkins Family Series (book 2)

Summer 2014 – *Legal Seduction*
Harlequin Kimani

**Turn the page for an excerpt of *All You'll Ever Need*
(Jada JJ Jenkins Story)
book 2 of the Jenkins Family Series**

ALL YOU'LL EVER NEED
BY SHARON C. COOPER

CHAPTER ONE

It is definitely raining men up in here. Jada Jenkins wove in and out of the small groups of people, stopping periodically to greet some of the wedding guests. She took special note of the handsome and hopefully single men in attendance at her cousin's reception.

"Girl, where did you find all of these gorgeous men?" Jada leaned in and whispered close to her cousin, Toni Jenkins-Logan's ear. Deafening music pumped through the speakers a couple of feet away, and made it hard for her to hear herself. She handed Toni a glass of Ginger Ale and claimed the seat next to her.

"You have Craig to thank for that," Toni answered and sipped from her drink. She squinted and scrunched up her face. "Goodness this soda is strong." A shiver skittered through her body and she took another small sip. "As for the gorgeous men, it turns out Craig has a lot of friends, and you'll be glad to know many of them are single."

"Hmm, that is good to know. I'll have to talk with my new cousin-in-law, but right now, I still can't believe you got married before me." Jada crossed her legs, her coral five-inch rhinestone embellished sandal dangled from her foot revealing the red bottom. "I'm the one who spends an arm and a leg making sure I look like someone from Life Styles of the Rich and Famous. Yet, you're the one who lands a Prince Charming. Hell, you didn't even want to get married."

Toni laughed. Her gaze landed on her new husband who stood across the banquet hall talking with a few of the groomsmen from their wedding only hours earlier. Jada didn't miss the way Toni's face lit up each time she glanced at Craig, and she couldn't ever remember seeing her cousin this happy.

"It's not that I didn't want to get married, I just never thought I ever would." Toni's gaze dropped to the table where she absently fingered a cloth napkin and then lifted her sparkling eyes to Jada. "This has been a long exhausting day, but it has been one of the best days of my life. I'm so excited that I get to spend the rest of my life with the most amazing man I've ever met. It's like a dream. Add having his baby to the mix and I feel as if I'm living someone else's fantasy life."

Jada reached over and squeezed Toni's hand. She was happy for Toni, or TJ as most of the Jenkins family called her, but she couldn't help but be a little envious. TJ was three months pregnant after believing she could never have children, and now she had married cutie-pie Craig Logan, an all-around great guy who was madly in love with her cousin. Jada wondered if she ever would experience the type of love and joy that radiated from Toni.

"I wish you years of happiness, Cuz."

"Thank you." Toni leaned over and hugged Jada. "And thanks for all you did pulling the wedding and reception together. Everything turned out wonderful."

Jada shrugged. "My pleasure. Just be ready for my big day, whenever that might be!" Jada returned her attention to the small group of men standing with Craig near the bar. "I guess it's true what they say. Beautiful people hang out together." All the men were as tall as Craig, at over six feet, and just as good looking in their black tuxedos sporting cummerbunds and bowties that matched the bridesmaid dresses.

"It looks that way, doesn't it?"

Jada nodded and then turned to Toni. "Okay, answer this, what do I have to do to get a man as *fine* as yours, one who worships the ground I walk on, but someone who is crazy wealthy?" She rolled her neck and slapped her hand down on the table. "I'm talkin' stinkin' rich as in lunch on the French Riviera and dinner at *La Vague d'Or* in Saint Tropez."

Toni shook her head, and a wide grin tilted the corners of her rose-colored lips. "I know suggesting that you lower your standard is out of the question. So I won't bother. I will say though, when the right man comes along, it's not going to matter if he's downright fine and stinkin' rich. All that's going to matter, or should matter is that he treats you right and loves you unconditionally."

"Uh, well, yeah, it *is* going to matter if he's fine and rich because if he isn't he won't be able to hang with me." Jada ignored the way Toni's perfectly arched eyebrows slanted in a frown. "Now what's the scoop on the hunks that just walked up to your new hubby? The one on the far right looks as if he could carry a small car on his back."

"Those are the guys he grew up with. Actually, today might be your lucky day." Toni perked up, a mischievous glint shined in her eyes as she adjusted the hem of her beaded lace wedding gown. "Craig's bringing Zack over."

"How does that make it my lucky day?"

"Because he's single and he's gawking at you."

Jada sized him up as he approached. At least six-one, broad shoulders that tapered down to a narrow waist, dark, spiked hair, and a powerful stride - he was a walking billboard for everything masculine. "Mmm, I don't think so. He's definitely a cutie in that Channing Tatum kind of way. But I like my men like I like my chocolate – dark and exceedingly rich."

"Is that right?" Toni placed her soda on the table and sat forward in her chair, her elbow on the table and amusement danced in her eyes. "Well, did I happen to mention that he's a professional football player who plays for the Cincinnati Cougars *and* has just renewed his contract for nine-point-five-million?"

Jada's mouth dropped wide open.

"Oh, and that's only for *one* year."

"*Damn!*" Jada smoothed down the front of her bridesmaid dress that stopped just above her knees and ran her fingers through her long auburn streaked curls. She quickly pulled a tube of lipstick from her strapless bra and ran the Coral Berry over her lips, and then took another glance at Craig's friend. "It's a good thing I'm switching over. I hear white chocolate, like milk, does a body good."

"What?" Toni narrowed her eyes. "I've never heard that before."

"Oh, hush up and tell me if I have any food in my teeth."

Toni shook her head and laughed. "Girl, you're a mess!"

"Hey, baby, are you feeling better?" Craig bent slightly and brushed Toni's bangs away from her forehead. "Did the soda help?" He extended his hand to help her to her feet and rubbed his large palm over her barely-there baby bump.

"Between the soda and the crackers you hunted down for me earlier, I'm feeling much better. You take such good care of me," Toni said in a baby-like voice.

"That's my job. I plan to spend the rest of my life taking very good care of you, Mrs. Logan." Craig lowered his head and his lips brushed against Toni's.

Jada rolled her eyes when the newlywed's lip-lock grew more intense and Toni's arms snaked around her husband's neck.

"You guys have a lifetime to play kissy-face." She turned her gaze to the man standing next to her cousin-in-law and had to admit he was even sexier up close, and then he smiled. *Oh my God he has dimples.* Her knees weakened and the once steady beat of her heart now pounded double-time. Her hand hovered over her chest as she struggled to fill her lungs with air. *Okay, just breathe.* She told herself over and over again.

"Are you all right?" the sexy gift from God asked, his hand at the small of her back sent a spark of desire shooting through her veins. "Can I get you something to drink?"

"Uh, no. No, I'm fine." She definitely had to pull herself together. Never has a man seen her sweat and she sure as hell wasn't going to let a cutie with a nine-point-five-million dollar contract see her off her game.

"Obviously we're invisible," Craig's friend said and removed his hand from her back. His voice intoxicatingly deep sent an exciting shiver up her spine. "I'm Zack Anderson."

Craig abruptly broke off the kiss with Toni. "Ah man, sorry you guys. Zack, this is Toni's cousin, JJ. I mean Jada Jenkins. JJ, this is one of my best friends, Zachary Anderson."

"Nice to meet you, Jada." Zack kissed the back of her hand and held on to it while he stared into her eyes. "I've heard some nice things about you."

Jada swallowed hard and tried to throttle the dizzying current that raced through her body. *What the hell?* She'd been in the midst of plenty of good-looking, wealthy men but never had one affected her like this. She eased her hand from his grasp and ran sweaty palms down the side of her dress as she regrouped, quickly plastering a flirtatious smile on her lips.

"Nice to meet you, Zachary."

"Please, call me Zack."

"Listen you two," Craig said from behind them, his arm around Toni. "My beautiful wife and I are going to greet our guest before the send off, and Zack," he leveled his friend with a pointed look, "behave yourself."

"I always do." Zack's piercing blue eyes roved and lazily appraised Jada, taking in all of her as if trying to memorize every intricate curve of her body.

Normally Jada would revolt against a man who openly gawked at her the way Zack was doing. Instead, she had the urge to stand perfectly still until he was done. *Damn, something is definitely wrong with me for enjoying the way he's sexing me up with his eyes.*

"Excuse me." Steven Jenkins, Jada's grandfather and the patriarch of the family jarred Jada out of her trance. He gave a quick nod to Zack before turning to her. "Your Highness, you're the only one of my granddaughters I haven't danced with yet. What do you say about cutting a rug with your old grandfather?"

"Oh, Grampa, there is nothing old about you and we don't say cutting a rug anymore. We just say dance." Jada grinned up at the man who had first given her the nickname Your Highness and the only man who had ever made her feel as if she were the most precious gift he'd ever received. Jada looped her arm through her grandfather's bent arm. "Stick with me. I'll keep you in the know."

He threw his head back and released a hearty laugh. "I don't know what I'm going to do with you."

Jada turned to Zack, still intrigued by the blue-eyed-dimpled god. "Grampa, I don't know if you've met Craig's friend Zack Anderson."

"Zack Anderson," Steven Jenkins repeated and extended his hand to Zack. "We haven't officially met, but of course I know you're one of the league's top-scoring running backs. I'm a big fan. Nice to meet you, I'm Steven Jenkins."

"It's a pleasure, sir." Zack shook his hand. "Craig mentions you and your family often in conversation. I'm glad to meet you and the other members of your family," he said to Mr. Jenkins, but his potent gaze wandered to Jada.

"Well a friend of Craig's is a friend of ours. Whenever the Cougars have a bye week, make sure you have Craig bring you to the house for Sunday brunch. We'd love to have you."

"I'd be honored." He bowed his head slightly and diverted his attention back to Jada.

She ignored the giddiness fluttering inside her stomach. "It was nice meeting you," she said, still awed by the dimples that winked at her each time he flashed his million-dollar smile. "Hopefully we'll get a chance to chat before the reception ends." She cast a gracious smile and batted her eyes knowing the combination of the two always got her what she wanted. And she definitely wanted to get to know Zachery Anderson better.

"It looks as if you have another admirer," Jada's grandfather commented as they danced to John Legend's latest release. "He's a hell of a football player, and he seems like a nice young man."

Jada glanced over her grandfather's shoulder at Zack whose enticing gaze held hers captive. "Yes he does seem like a nice young man, doesn't he?"

***

Zack stared at Jada and her grandfather as they twirled around the dance floor in perfect sync. *She sure as hell doesn't look like any sheet metal worker I've ever seen.* Intoxicating brown eyes that hinted of mischief and lips that were designed for kissing left him mesmerized.

He first spotted her at the church and immediately found her captivating. At five-feet-five with full breasts, curvy hips, and long toned legs, it was no wonder the men in attendance couldn't take their gaze off of her. The gracefulness of her stroll down the aisle and the gentle sway in which her hips moved in the fitted bridesmaid dress was hypnotic. Thankfully the Cougars were playing in town this weekend, otherwise he would have missed the wedding altogether. Craig had mentioned the Jenkins family, and the granddaughters who oversaw the day-to-day operations of Jenkins & Sons Construction, but he was going to have to talk to his long-time friend. The way Craig described the stunning Jenkins women hadn't done Jada justice.

Zack watched as the elder Jenkins moved his granddaughter smoothly across the dance floor as if dancing was something they did together all the time.

"She's way out of your league man. Besides, I can look at her and tell she's high maintenance and everyone knows how you feel about high maintenance women," Donny Caldron, a friend of Zack and Craig's from the old neighborhood said, and lifted his glass to his lips.

"Nah, I don't think she's high maintenance." Zack continued to observe her on the dance floor. He smiled to himself. She seemed to put a little extra hip action in her moves each time her grandfather released her hand. "She definitely has some sass, but I bet she's a real sweetheart once you get to know her, which I plan to do."

"Okay, so which one is she anyway? The carpenter? The electrician?"

"That's Jada. Can you believe she's a sheet metal worker?"

"Nope, but I can't believe any of them work construction. They make me want to tear down a house, just so I can have them build it back up, brick by tantalizing brick."

Zack threw his head back, and his laugh rippled through the room. While growing up, Donny was always the one who kept everyone laughing. With his laid-back attitude, many people would be surprised to know that he was the CEO for one of the city's largest pharmaceutical companies.

Zack shoved his hands into his pants pockets and rocked on the balls of his feet. "Well, I don't plan on tearing anything down. All I need is one date with her and she'll be mine."

Donny fell out laughing. "I think you've had one too many knocks upside the head out there on that football field because you're definitely talking crazy. That woman is not going out with your country ass," he joked. "Besides, I thought that since you're looking to retire next year you wanted to meet someone to settle down with. If that's still the case, you need to look elsewhere. She's not the one"

Donny always called him country despite the fact that they all grew up in Columbus, Ohio. "I'm no more country than you are and why do you think she's not the one for me? I beg to differ. Since she's a sheet metal worker, she clearly doesn't mind getting her hands dirty. I bet she's the outdoorsy type and enjoys hiking, biking and probably even fishing. Hell, she's exactly the type of woman I've been looking for - someone who's not too prissy to wear an old pair of jeans and a T-shirt, but someone who cleans up well and is classy enough to wow my family and friends."

Donny's brows drew together as he shook his head. "Apparently we're looking at two different women. I would bet my paycheck that the woman you just describe is nowhere near the woman we're watching dance with the old dude. I don't care how many women have told you how *fine* you are or how many cater to your every desire once they find out how much you're worth. You don't stand a chance with her man. She's too much woman for you."

"Whatever, dude." Zack nudged him in the shoulder. "Why don't we put a wager on whether or not she'll go out with me?" He removed a wad of money from his front pocket and started counting off bills.

"Man, you know I hate taking your money." Donny smirked. "But if you insist. I bet you a thousand bucks she turns your ass down cold."

"Yeah, we'll see about that."

***

"Grampa I'm impressed," Jada said. "You still have some moves. You're putting these young dudes to shame."

"Hey, I have to be able to keep up with all you kids." He spun her around and then pulled her back into his arms. "Your grandmother and I haven't seen you lately. What have you been up to?"

"Working. Grampa, I know you put Peyton in charge for a reason, but that girl has been working me like a slave." Her cousin Peyton (PJ) Jenkins was an electrician by trade and the senior construction manager for Jenkins & Sons Construction. "Do you know how many times I had to get my manicure touched up this week? Three times," Jada said without giving him a chance to respond. "I am so ready to find a wealthy husband, quit my job, and live happily-ever-after."

"Sweetheart, are you sure you're ready for marriage?"

She leaned away from her grandfather and frowned. "You know I am Grampa. I'm sick of working and don't get me started on taking out my own trash and making repairs around the condo. I'm tired of doing everything for myself, and more importantly, I'm sick of the dating scene. I want to marry someone who is crazy in love with me and enjoys taking me out on the town. And Grampa, did you see this scar on my face?" She slowed her steps and pointed to the one-inch scratch under her jaw, near her chin. "I can't afford to get any more marks on my body from lugging sheet metal around all day."

Her grandfather hesitated and Jada groaned. She dropped her head on his shoulder, regretting all that she'd shared, knowing she had just earned herself one of his famous lectures. Before she could retract her statement, he spoke.

"Your Highness, I know we have spoiled you and led you to believe that the world revolves around you, but let me explain something." He spun her around and then pulled her back into his arms. "It's not all about you. When some lucky young man finds *you*, and not the other way around, your main goal should be making sure that he's the man you want to spend the rest of your life with, not the man who can buy you the latest Hermès Birkin handbag."

"I know Grampa," Jada responded, surprised her grandfather knew anything about Hermès.

"Do you?" He slowed his steps and pulled back. His eyes narrowed and his gaze bored into her. "Because what I'm hearing from you is a lot of me, me, me, but sweetheart marriage takes work. Your parents, and your grandmother and I, might make marriage look easy, but we work hard to make our relationship work. Life, and marriage for that matter, is not like Burger King, you can't always have it your way."

Jada shook her head and laughed. "I know Grampa. Don't worry I get what you're saying." She wrapped her arms around his neck and placed a kiss on his cheek.

"When my Mr. Right comes along, I'll remember not to make everything all about me."

It was then she noticed Zack heading her way and her breath caught at his seductive, confident gait. *Mercy, this man personifies sexy.*

"Excuse me. May I cut in?"

***All You'll Ever Need* – Available April 2014**

CPSIA information can be obtained at www.ICGtesting.com
Printed in the USA
LVOW07s1223200715

446887LV00001B/36/P